Readers love *Ropea*
by SJD PETERSON

"I truly adore Jo Peterson, definitely as a person, but she constantly blows me away with her writing. *Roped* is book four in her Guards of Folsom series and each book I think "There's no way she can meet or exceed the previous book". But, each time, she does, and I believe I'm going to stop wondering how she does it. I have certain authors that no matter what they write, be it romance, paranormal, contemporary, urban fantasy, or a combination of all, I always enjoy their work. SJD Peterson is one of those authors."

—Rainbow Book Alliance

"Jo Peterson, in my opinion has showed her versatility as a writer in this instalment from The Guards of Folsom series and moved in a completely different direction which I personally found immensely rewarding as a reader. She never fails to grab my attention and keep me enthralled, I didn't think it could get any better but, Jo has proved me wrong."

—Sinfully Sexy Book Reviews

"I found this story really intriguing and I can't wait to see how the future comes together for Tck and Jamie."

—Joyfully Jay

"I will be the first in line to buy the next book in the series because I can't wait to find out what the author has in store for the Tek and Jamie and all the rest of the men of Folsom."

—Love Bytes

By SJD PETERSON

BAMF
Beyond Duty
Leon
Masters & Boyd
Plan B
Tuck & Cover

GUARDS OF FOLSOM
Riveted
Pup
Tag Team
Pony
Roped

WHISPERING PINES RANCH
Lorcan's Desire
Quinn's Need
Ty's Obsession
Conner's Courage
Jess's Journey

Published by DREAMSPINNER PRESS
http://www.dreamspinnerpress.com

BAMF

SJD PETERSON

Dreamspinner Press

Published by
DREAMSPINNER PRESS

5032 Capital Circle SW, Suite 2, PMB# 279, Tallahassee, FL 32305-7886 USA
http://www.dreamspinnerpress.com/

BAMF
© 2014 SJD Peterson.

Cover Art
© 2014 Reese Dante.
http://www.reesedante.com.
Cover content is for illustrative purposes only and any person depicted on the cover is a model.

ISBN: 978-1-62798-902-2
Digital ISBN: 978-1-62798-903-9
Library of Congress Control Number: 2014940024
First Edition July 2014

Printed in the United States of America

This paper meets the requirements of
ANSI/NISO Z39.48-1992 (Permanence of Paper).

To Scott, thanks for the great one-liners.

CHAPTER 1

RIDLEY CORBIN was the protector of the underdog, a role he'd come into as a direct product of his upbringing. A squirrely little kid, he had buckteeth, bright red hair, and was a good ten pounds and two inches shorter than the next smallest kid. A runt, and an ugly one at that, he'd been bullied nearly every day of his first three years at Gates Elementary School.

During those early days, he'd drop to his knees next to his bed and beg God for a little brother or sister. It would have been cool to have had a sibling to play with—even if he or she were forced to play with him by their mom. Apparently something had gone wrong during his birth, though, and they'd had to pull out Mom's baby box. But hey, at least the prayers had been good for something—he got a puppy.

The summer between third and fourth grade, Ridley thought he'd gotten the next best thing to a sibling. Brock Hanners moved into the house next to his, and Ridley thought that, since they were the only two kids on the cul-de-sac, Brock would want to play with him. He was wrong.

Brock was huge; well, at least to Ridley's scrawny little ass he was. Much to his dismay, Brock bullied him too. He used to steal Ridley's bike, take his toys, even came over once and knocked down his clubhouse. Granted it was only a couple of kitchen chairs and old blankets and he was the only member, but it was his. Instead of the friend he had hoped for, Ridley found himself even more miserable after Brock moved in. He was being picked on at school and now bullied at home as well.

However, Ridley was a smart kid and Brock, well, he wasn't too bright. Brock had been held back a couple of years—hence why he was so much bigger than everyone else. So when classes resumed in the fall, they came to a little agreement. Ridley would do Brock's homework and Brock would keep Ridley safe at school. Brock was like his own personal bodyguard. Not a perfect arrangement, but he learned some great study habits doing the work of two, and it saved him a crap-ton of ass beatings.

Brock moved away during their junior year of high school, but by then Ridley had had his teeth fixed, his hair had changed from Bozo red to a nice chestnut color, and, most importantly, he'd grown. He was still scrawny, but he was inching up on six feet and had a wicked bank shot.

It would have been easy to become one of those kids who felt that just because he'd been bullied his whole life, it was now his turn to be the bully. Instead, he became more like Brock, except Ridley did it for free and he was a lot smarter. Okay, he was nothing like Brock. He never took advantage of someone and he'd never failed a class, but he did take to the protector part.

So it was only natural that he was on the move as soon as he heard Kyle Bouche's familiar sneer—*Hey, nerd boy. Where can I find a book on Gustave Courbet?*—on the other side of the books he was searching through. Damn, he hated that guy. Kyle was the big man at Slater University. Quarterback for the football team, student body president, as well as president of his fraternity, blah, blah, blah. Ridley didn't normally pay attention to the shit that went on around the campus, couldn't care less. He kept his head down, stayed to himself, and worked hard to keep his grade point average at a 4.0. The only reason he knew about Kyle's activities was because the fucker liked to brag about them. Personally, Ridley thought Kyle was a complete and utter dickhead.

Ridley eased his way around the aisle, and there in the next row was Kyle, smirking at Alex Firestone. Ridley was about to step in and teach Kyle a few manners, but stopped when he saw Alex glare at Kyle and say, "Look it up on the computer like everyone else." Alex then went back to sorting the books in his cart.

Ridley tensed and his hands tightened on the Truman Capote's *In Cold Blood* he was holding as Kyle moved up close to Alex. Kyle puffed his chest up in an obvious attempt to intimidate Alex. The idea made Ridley crazy and he wanted so badly to slap Kyle up against his thick head. The little bantam rooster had no idea who he was messing with. Yes, Ridley fancied himself protector of the underdog, but with Alex the need was even sharper. It was personal. If Kyle laid so much as a finger on Alex, Kyle would be washing the cold blood from his face later. Ridley had to bite down on his lip to keep from laughing at the irony.

"Do you have any idea who you're talking to?" Kyle snarled.

Ridley shifted slightly, fighting back the urge to pounce when Kyle put the cart between him and Alex and leaned in close. He couldn't see Kyle's face but clearly saw the narrowed gaze and challenging look Alex gave him in return.

"Yeah, you're the guy who is going to use the computer to search for your book like everyone else," Alex informed Kyle without so much as flinching.

Alex worked in the library, and although Ridley didn't really have a need to be in the library—with his major in mechanical engineering, most of his studies were done hands-on or on the computer—he found himself drawn there anyway. Basically he was there to gawk at the star of his wet dreams, Alex Firestone. No, he wasn't a freaky stalker. He just hadn't built up the nerve to approach the sexy man. Okay, it might have been bordering on stalkerish since he'd been doing quite a bit of gawking over the last six months, but damn, it was Alex Firestone.

Alex was the same six-foot height, and although he tended to wear dress shirts and slacks that were a bit big for him, Ridley could tell Alex had an impressive build beneath the cotton material. He also had the most amazing gunmetal-blue eyes Ridley had ever seen. Oh, and then there was the fact that Alex had a head full of unruly blond curls and the biggest and sweetest dimples ever. He also wore heavy-framed black glasses, and the bow ties he sported were just too adorable for words. Basically, Alex worked the fuck out of cute.

Miss Fenton pushed past Ridley and snapped at Kyle, "Can I help you, young man?"

Alex didn't so much as blink nor take his gaze from Kyle as the librarian stepped up to them with her hands on her wide hips. Ridley suspected Alex knew Kyle was a fucking coward and would probably attempt to sucker punch him if he looked away. Alex wasn't only adorable, he was smart, a combination Ridley found very appealing. Fake alphas like Kyle Bouche, with all their posturing and crowing, usually played dirty. Ridley knew the kind all too well and he was actually hoping the egotistical bastard was stupid enough to try something. It had been a while since he'd thrown down and he was itching for a good fight. The idea of doing it to protect Alex, earn a few brownie points with the man, was all the more appealing.

"I said, can I help you, young man?" Miss Fenton asked again as she stepped up closer still. "Oh, Kyle, I didn't recognize you. How are you, son?" Her tone instantly went from angry to sickly sweet once she recognized whom she was talking to.

For a long, tense moment, Kyle didn't move nor did Alex take his eyes from him, but when Kyle finally turned to Miss Fenton, there was a fake smile plastered on his face. "I'm great, Miss Fenton. Wow, you're looking good. Is that a new haircut?"

Miss Fenton was about a hundred years old—or at least she looked as if she were—never married—big shocker there—and was as wide as she was tall. Not to mention she had a reputation for being a raging bitch—something Ridley had personally witnessed—so Kyle's compliment was like everything else about the man, fake.

"Oh, you little charmer, you," Miss Fenton giggled. "Now what can I help you with?"

Kyle laced his arm in Miss Fenton's and pulled her along. "Aww, sweetie, you've already helped with putting a smile on my face with your presence. But if you could point me in the direction of where I can find a book on Gustave Courbet, I'd much appreciate it."

Ridley shook his head when he heard Miss Fenton giggle again and offer to escort Kyle to the correct location. Hundred-year-old mummies with nasty dispositions should never, ever giggle, nor should one try to make them. It was just—Ridley shuddered—gross. Kyle may be a major shit, but he was a hell of an impressive actor. There was no way in hell Ridley could smooth talk the cranky ol' bat. Obviously, Kyle didn't care what kind of person someone was as long as he got his way. Kyle was the kind of douchebag who'd sleep with the walking mummy if he thought he'd get an advancement of some sort. Ridley shuddered again.

Alex watched Kyle and Miss Fenton until they disappeared before he returned to his work. Ridley watched with astonishment as he finished shelving the last couple books from the cart. The man wasn't only cute, smart, and had a sexy ass, he was brave. Alex seemed to be the kind of guy who didn't back down or let bullies intimidate him, even if at a disadvantage. Alex definitely tripped all Ridley's triggers.

When Alex met Ridley's gaze as he moved down the aisle, he grinned and shrugged. Ridley could only nod in response. It was on the tip of his tongue to ask Alex out, say something, anything, but Ridley's mouth was dry and he couldn't get anything out past his restricted throat. Christ, Alex got him all tongue-tied and feeling like an awkward school boy with just one look. Once again, Ridley failed to grab hold of a perfect opportunity to talk to the man. Instead he stood there like a complete knob.

Frustrated, Ridley took his book and headed to the large open area with plenty of workstations. He scanned the area; most of the tables were occupied by students with their noses in textbooks.

Brittney looked up at him and batted her lashes. "Hi, Ridley," she whispered and waved.

Ridley swallowed down his groan. He didn't know Brittney's last name, although she'd told him several times, he just didn't care. He gave her a curt nod and kept moving. He was normally friendly with most people, but he'd learned not to engage Brittney a few months prior. While she was cute, even if a little nerdy, she was annoying as hell. She was always twirling her mousey brown hair in her fingers, popping her gum, and good lord the girl could talk, and fast. He'd lost the gist of the conversation more than once while he stared at her, trying to figure out when the hell she would take a breath. It seemed like she could chatter for hours without taking one.

Ridley took a seat as far from Brittney as he could and opened his book, flipping through the pages without looking at them, keeping an eye out for Alex. He caught one man sitting at the far end staring back at him with a suspicious expression on his face. Ridley waved and smiled charmingly. The guy instantly looked away. He got that a lot. People got a glimpse of his heavily tattooed arms and facial piercings and assumed he was a thug. Or maybe he stood out more in this environment because he rarely—okay, never—brought a backpack, notebook, or pen to give the appearance of doing any kind of research or actual homework. Instead he always grabbed a random book, flipped through it without ever reading a single word, and watched Alex. Now that he thought about it, he really was totally a freaky stalker.

An hour later Ridley was still flipping through the pages of the same book when he noticed Alex grab his coat and shrug it on as he headed for the main entrance. Not only had Ridley spent his time checking Alex out every chance he got, but he'd also been having a bit of a talk with his inner chickenshit. He wasn't used to dealing with that part of himself. Once he'd overcome his rough elementary years, Ridley had grown into a pretty confident guy. He'd never had an issue with his sexuality, nor had he ever been afraid to approach a guy before. Again, his only excuse was this was Alex Firestone, the most amazing fucking man he'd ever laid eyes on. Still, Ridley was able to wrestle down the nerves, pop a mint to help with the dry mouth and throat, and chase after Alex.

"Hey, Alex."

Alex stopped on the stone steps outside the library and looked back at Ridley with a wary look.

"It is Alex, isn't it?" Ridley asked with a grin. Of course he knew his name, but it was the only thing he could come up with to get Alex talking. Actually, Ridley was pretty fucking proud he'd gotten that much out, considering the fact that his stomach was churning and he was so goddamn nervous he wanted to puke.

"Yeah," Alex responded hesitantly. "Do I know you?"

He held out his hand. "Ridley Corbin."

The instant Alex placed his hand in Ridley's, he swore he felt sparks. When Alex shook it, that little spark ignited and heat rushed through Ridley.

"Do I know you?" Alex asked again.

"No, we've never met," Ridley said with a shake of his head. "I've noticed you a couple of times on campus and I asked around until I found out your name," he lied, sort of.

It was a hell of a lot more than a couple of times, but Ridley wasn't about to tell Alex he'd noticed him a few hundred. How creepy would that sound? After the struggle he'd had finding the courage to approach Alex, Ridley sure as hell didn't want the guy running and screaming, or worse, taking out a personal protection order against him. Ridley tried his best to give Alex his most charming smile but wasn't sure if he pulled it off. Alex's eyes narrowed as he stared at Ridley's mouth. Hopefully it was the silver ring in his bottom lip that caught Alex's eye and not something stuck between his teeth.

"You didn't need the stealth tactics. You could have just asked me what my name was." Alex's grin turned sly. "You know, during one of all those times you were in the library."

Oh damn, busted. Only Alex's gaze wandered down Ridley's body appreciatively, and it caused some of the nervousness to seep away. Apparently he was intrigued and Ridley hoped that meant he was interested.

"I was just heading over to the diner to grab a bite to eat. Care to join me?" Ridley offered.

"Thanks for the invite, but I've got something I have to take care of," Alex said with a shrug.

It would have been nice to take Alex to dinner, spend a little time getting to know him, but Ridley didn't dare push too hard, and he sure as hell didn't want to sound desperate. "Okay, maybe another time?" Ridley asked hopefully.

"Sure," Alex responded with what sounded like sincerity, but then he turned his back and tossed over his shoulder, "See you around."

Alex tromped down the steps, and Ridley struggled to find something to say, unwilling to let Alex get away just yet. "Wait," he called out and hurried down the stairs to catch up. "I couldn't help but notice the way Kyle was fucking with you. You have any problems with that asshole, don't hesitate to let me know, okay?"

"Thanks. I'll be sure to let you know if I need a knight in shining armor," Alex said with a wink.

"Let me give you my number." Ridley patted his pockets. *Shit!* "Got a pen?"

Alex pulled one from inside his coat and handed it to him. Ridley patted his pockets again like he thought a notebook would have magically appeared in the two seconds since the last time he'd checked them. Before thinking it through, he grabbed Alex's hand and wrote his number across his palm and then opened Alex's coat and slid the pen back into the pocket of his dress shirt. "Talk to you soon, Alex," he said with as much confidence as he could muster.

Alex cocked his head and looked at him with a strange expression on his face. Ridley would have given just about anything to know what he was thinking. It was a struggle not to squirm under Alex's scrutiny, but somehow he managed. In fact, it was a major fucking relief when Alex finally nodded and with a smile said, "Yeah, talk to you soon."

Ridley stood there, no doubt drool dripping from his chin as he watched Alex walk away. His pert butt swayed with each step he took, holding Ridley's attention. He liked the way Alex moved, his sexy-as-hell swagger was fucking hypnotic, and Ridley's body heated further, a tingling sensation settling into his groin. It had been a while since he'd been laid, and after all the time he'd spent fantasizing about Alex, it was getting to the point where even a slight breeze would cause his dick to perk up.

Alex disappeared into the crowd at the end of the block, and then Ridley stuffed his hands into the pockets of his coat and headed in the opposite direction. He whistled as he walked, avoiding eye contact with anyone, ever aware of the ache between his legs. A man could only ignore the needs of his body for so long. He was getting tired of spending all his nights with nothing more than thoughts of Alex, a bottle of lube, and his right hand for companionship.

It wasn't just the previous six months he'd been stalking—checking out—Alex since he'd been laid. He'd moved from southern California to Slater more than a year prior, having been awarded a full-ride scholarship. Slater was a small town located in the upper peninsula of Michigan and didn't have a lot to offer outside the tiny university. Much to Ridley's dismay, he learned soon after arriving in Slater that the town was completely lacking in any kind of nightlife. Ridley had never considered a study group or sporting events a form of satisfying entertainment. The closest dance club was thirty miles away, and during the winter months, it may as well have been three thousand.

He'd always enjoyed a very... *fulfilling* sex life before he left home. He'd always been insatiable, and dammit, he wanted a fucking blow job at the very least. Having someone who looked like Alex consuming his thoughts made the unfilled desires all the more intolerable. Somehow he had to not only convince Alex to go out with him, but get that sexy fucker in his bed.

CHAPTER 2

RIDLEY HAD accepted the fact that he was becoming a wee bit obsessed with Alex, definitely bordering on becoming that creepy stalker dude. He didn't want to be *that* guy, so as hard as it was, he stayed away from the library for an entire week after giving Alex his number. Neither the realization of obsession nor his resolve did little to curb his new obsession—checking his phone every five seconds.

Thinking a full seven days would be a sufficient waiting period, Ridley showed back up at the library. Actually, seven days was all he could stand. He was jonesing to see Alex again, and there was no fucking way he could stay away another day. With a new haircut, shaved close on the sides, the top styled into a fauxhawk, and a ten-spot shelled out to have his beard trimmed nice and close, he pushed through the doors and instantly scanned the area for his lust interest. He'd also sprung for a new silver ring to replace the black bar in his eyebrow as well as matching hoops in both his ears. He was totally styling and looking damn fine, if he said so himself. Ridley just hoped Alex would appreciate the shit he'd gone through, not to mention the money he'd spent to look good for him.

He spotted Alex leaning against the front counter. Although his back was to Ridley, he'd know that mess of blond curls anywhere. What stopped him dead in his tracks and caused his heart to race like a runaway locomotive was what Alex was wearing. Previously, Ridley had only assumed Alex had a nice, athletic body, but it had been difficult to be one hundred percent certain with how baggy his clothes were. Now he knew exactly how impressive Alex's lean, muscular body was by the way his skinny jeans clung to his well-developed thighs and pert little butt. His tight blue T-shirt showed off his broad shoulders and was tucked into jeans at his narrow waist. Christ on a stick, the man wasn't just gorgeous, he was a fucking god! And there Ridley was, popping a boner standing in the entryway and not even caring about the strange looks people were tossing at him or the way they sidestepped him.

Ridley pulled his shirt out of his suddenly overly tight jeans and stepped up to the counter next to Alex. "Oh, hi," he greeted in mock surprise.

"Hi. Ridley, right?" Alex asked.

He was ridiculously happy that Alex had remembered his name and smiled broadly, all the while trying to act calm and cool, like it was no big thing. But in his head he was screaming, *Yes! Yes! Alex Fucking Firestone remembered my name!* Damn, he was pathetic.

"Yeah, that's right. How have you been?" Ridley responded with as much nonchalance as he could muster. He wasn't sure how it looked, but at least his voice came out steady and didn't squeak.

"Good. I meant to call you, but by the time I got home, your number was smudged. I've been watching for you."

"Seriously?" he said excitedly and a bit too loudly. He quickly clamped down on his excitement, turned, and went to rest his elbow on the counter and… yeah, missed the whole smooth-operator thing when he practically fell on his ass when his traitorous trembling knees buckled.

"Whoa there," Alex said and grabbed onto Ridley's arm to keep him upright. "You okay?"

Ridley briefly thought of lying and telling Alex he had low blood sugar and hadn't eaten, or he had a rare disease that caused him to get excited randomly, but while he was searching through and discarding lies, he found himself saying, "I'm fine. I get a little flustered when I'm around you." *Shit!* Where the hell had that come from or rather, *why the fuck did I say it*? Ridley turned away from Alex, set his elbow on the counter, and rested his forehead against his palm, his embarrassment complete. "I didn't mean to say that out loud," he admitted.

"I thought it was cute." Alex grinned.

Ridley glanced at him out of the corner of his eye. "Wow. Way to kick a man when he's down," he muttered playfully.

"What? It *was* cute." Alex laughed and Ridley wouldn't have thought it possible, but damn if it didn't make Alex all the sexier.

"Cute, huh?" Ridley arched a brow. "You're going to have to make that up to me, ya know?"

"Well, if you were hoping I'd replace your man card with mine, sorry but I lost mine a hundred"—Alex made the universal symbol for quotation marks—"*cute* remarks ago."

"Guess you'll just have to have dinner with me, then," Ridley informed him, feeling a little more confident. "You know, for stripping me of my card."

"Here you go," said a little redhead, handing Alex a large manila envelope.

"Thanks, Amanda," Alex said with a grin and took the envelope. He tucked it under his arm and then turned to Ridley. "Okay, when?"

It took him a minute to catch up, or maybe he was in shock that Alex actually said yes, because Ridley stood there with his mouth gaping, staring like a deer caught in headlights. He was batting a thousand for the dork squad. Thankfully, Amanda gave him a helping hand by distracting Alex.

"Any chance you can cover my shift on Saturday? I have a date," she asked.

"Anyone I know?" Alex responded.

The two of them chatted about schedules and some guy named Kevin that Alex didn't seem to like too much, but Ridley wasn't really paying attention. Since he was pretty sure he'd heard Alex say "okay," Ridley was taking the opportunity to take some deep breaths, slow his racing heart, and doing his fucking damnedest not to break out into some kind of lame happy dance. He'd already embarrassed himself enough, and with his no-rhythm ass jerking and twitching around, Alex would have been screaming and running from the crazy or falling to the floor with laughter.

"Did you need anything?"

"Oh... um, no, I'm good," Ridley told Amanda. It was a bit delayed, but he caught up quickly when she cocked her head and gave him a funny look.

"Alrighty, then," she muttered. "See you later, Alex."

Alex waved to Amanda and then turned to Ridley. "So, when?"

"No time like the present," Ridley said smoothly, having gotten a little control of his giddiness.

"Dude," Alex chuckled, checking his watch. "It's just after nine in the morning."

"I'm sure it's noon somewhere in the world. Besides," Ridley said with a shrug. "I've never been one to follow the rules."

"Is that so?" With the glint in his eyes, Alex looked like he was laughing at Ridley, just a little. "I have some things to take care of this morning. How about we meet up at two at the pub on Main?"

"That works. See you then!"

Ridley made a beeline for the front door. Seriously, he needed to get the hell out of there because the jerking and twitching dance was getting nearly impossible to contain much longer. He stopped with his hand on the door and looked over his shoulder. Alex was leaning against the counter, his eyes on him. Ridley waved and stepped out of the library, but once again he had the feeling that his lust interest was laughing. Ridley wasn't sure if that boded well for him or not. Whatever. He had a date and had less than five hours to get his shit together and see if he could fish out his backup man card.

IT TOOK every bit of the time he had to primp. He had the craziest fucking hair. It should have been easy to style since the sides were shaved and it had just been cut and styled earlier that day. But after a long, hot shower with extra time for meticulous manscaping, he was left struggling with all the fancy hair products the stylist had given him. No matter how many times he tried to duplicate what the stylist had done, he couldn't seem to get it right. His fauxhawk kept ending up looking like a limphawk. The third time he washed it, he was starting to worry all the crap he was adding to it, the heat of the blow dryer, straight iron, blah, blah, blah, was going to leave him permanently bald. He ended up calling his best friend Rae.

"I'm here! What's wrong," Rae said by way of greeting when she rushed through the door.

"Help," Ridley pleaded while holding up the hair glue and spray.

"You have got to be fucking kidding me, Ridley," she grumbled and snatched the products away. "You sounded panicked. I thought there was something seriously wrong."

"There is. Look at this crap," he countered and pointed to his hair. "I have a date in less than an hour."

"You made me rush over here for your hair?" Rae slapped his arm.

"Ow, stop beating on me and start helping," he groaned and plopped down in the chair. "And stop being so damn dramatic. You make it sound like you had to rush across town rather than down the hall."

"Yeah, well," she said and rolled her eyes. "Ever think I might have been doing something important?"

"No, now start styling."

"Tell me again why you're my best friend?" she quipped as she started putting the sticky stuff in his hair.

"So you can pass math."

"Oh, right," she chuckled. "So let me guess, you have a date with Mr. Hot and Geeky?"

"What makes you think that?" he demurred.

"Because you've been talking about him for months and he's the only person you'd get this freaked over your hair for."

"Yeah, whatever." But he wasn't fooling Rae. She had had to listen to him go on about Alex once or a thousand times. He felt no guilt or shame. He'd had to listen to her going on and on and on about some guy in her economics class. They were even.

Rae ran her fingers through his hair for a minute and then exclaimed, "All done."

"No way!" He jumped up and ran to the mirror. How in the hell had she done that so quickly? It was perfect.

"Time to work on your clothes."

"My clothes?" Ridley looked down at the black T-shirt and jeans he was wearing and then at Rae with wide eyes. "Oh shit! I don't look good, do I?" Ridley asked, panic beginning to cause his gut to flutter, and not at all pleasantly.

"Good thing you have me," she reminded him and started pulling shit from the closet. "Now about my payment."

By the time Ridley slid into the booth at Jake's Pub twenty minutes before two, he didn't even care how deeply in debt to Rae he was. Even the nightmare of having to escort her to the ballet version of *Romeo and Juliet* would be worth it. Confession—he hated the ballet. Although, he'd have endured worse than spending a couple hours watching guys in tights with bulging packages hop around if that was what it took to make her happy. She not only made sure his hair was perfect, she had also helped dress him and prevented more than one freak-the-fuck-out meltdown.

He was calm, cool, collected, and looking super fine, sipping on a pint of craft brew—and then he spotted Alex walking through the front door. Instantly his heart began to race, and he choked on his mouthful of beer. Damn, if he hadn't chosen his seat perfectly because by the time Alex spotted him and headed over to the booth, he had stopped coughing and wiped away the beer that had run down his chin. He couldn't do anything about the speed of his heart or the butterflies going nuts in his gut, but at least his voice was strong and even when he said, "Hi, Alex."

"Hi," Alex replied with a smile as he slid into the booth across from Ridley and waved toward the waiter. "How've you been?"

A complete and utter fucking mess. "I'm good. How was your day?"

"Productive," Alex responded and winked. "Can I get a pint of Guinness?" he asked the waiter.

"Sure. You ready for another?" the server asked Ridley, pointing to his nearly empty mug.

Ridley downed the rest of his beer and handed him the mug.

"Thanks for inviting me," Alex commented, glancing around the room. "I've been meaning to check this place out. It's cool."

"You've never been here?" Ridley asked with true shock.

Jake's Pub was the only place in town to get a beer, play pool, and just hang out. Well, there were the First Presbyterian Church, the post office, and the organic deli to hang out at, but he just couldn't picture Alex in any of those places. The pub fit him, so it was all the more unbelievable that he had never been there.

"Nope," Alex responded after thanking the waiter for the beers. "I don't really get out much."

"Well, then, I feel all the more special for you accepting my invitation." He lifted his mug and Alex clinked his against it.

They both took long pulls of their brews. Ridley's gaze was drawn to Alex's throat and his Adam's apple bobbing as he swallowed. Ridley couldn't help it, he imagined Alex swallowing down other things, hard things, intimate things. A tingling sensation ran across his groin, and he knew he needed to keep his naughty thoughts in check or he'd be embarrassing himself once again in the form of a wet spot on the front of his jeans.

"So what do you do for fun?" Ridley inquired, needing the subject changed. He prayed Alex didn't say fucking or BAM, soggy jeans.

"Between my work and school schedule, I don't really have much time for fun," Alex admitted.

"You know that old saying, all work and no play makes Alex a—"

"I'm far from a dull boy," Alex interrupted with a smirk. "I simply needed to take a bit of a"—he waved his hand dismissively—"break from all the fun."

"The chess club knows how to party, huh?" Ridley teased.

"You have no idea," Alex muttered.

For a split second there was a look of regret in Alex's eyes that was in sharp contrast to the easy smile on his face. It was gone before Ridley could be sure, but it made him think there was a bit more to Alex than just a cute library assistant and college student. Ridley wasn't sure why he felt that way from such a fleeting look, it was just a feeling he had. More astonishingly, that one look made him realize he didn't want to just fuck the guy, he wanted to know everything about him, including what had caused the regret.

"So what's your area of study?" Ridley asked as he ran his finger along the condensation on his mug.

"Accounting and financial management. Shocked?"

Ridley couldn't help but laugh and shake his head. "No, not really."

Given Alex's appearance, it didn't surprise him at all. However, he was quickly learning not to assume anything when it came to Alex.

"What about you? Wait, let me guess," Alex amended and tapped his finger against the table as he studied Ridley.

Ridley did his best not to fidget under the scrutiny, but it was tough. He liked having Alex's eyes on him, liked the thoughtful expression on his face. Ridley sipped his beer, keeping his gaze locked with Alex's.

"I got it! You're studying to be a rocket scientist."

It burned like hell as beer shot out his nose when he choked on a laugh. Ridley set his mug aside and grabbed his napkin. "Fucker," he grumbled as he wiped the beer and snot from his face.

"That was entertaining." Alex chuckled. "I take it I didn't guess correctly," he commented smugly.

"Yeah…. No. Mechanical engineering." Ridley threw the napkin at Alex, who snatched it out of the air easily. Ridley cocked his head at him. "Impressive reflexes."

"What? You're surprised a geek can be as good with his hands as he is with his brain?" Alex crumpled the napkin and tossed it aside.

"One can only hope," Ridley murmured wryly into his beer. He was actually thinking a sexy-ass geek with talented hands would be a dream come true. The only thing that would make it more perfect would be if said sexy-ass geek with talented hands was also a kinky top. Of course he hoped for it all, but as he looked over at Alex, Ridley highly doubted he'd have an issue compromising. With someone who looked like Alex, Ridley figured he might even learn to prefer having Alex beneath him instead of in him.

"What was that?"

"Can I get you another beer?" Ridley offered and pointed at his empty mug.

"Mmmhmm," Alex hummed and pushed the mug toward Ridley.

The beers flowed as easily as the laughter over the next couple of hours. Ridley didn't really learn a lot about Alex other than he was twenty-four and didn't like to talk about himself, his family, or his past. Ridley was hoping to change that over a game of pool. And hey, if not, Ridley could think of worse ways to spend the evening than watching Alex bend over to take a shot.

"You want to break?" Ridley offered as he slid the quarters into the table and dropped the balls.

"Sure. Although I should warn you, I suck at pool when I'm stone-cold sober. But drunk…." Alex shrugged one shoulder.

"That's okay. I'll take it easy on you," Ridley offered with a wink.

Ridley racked the balls while Alex chalked up his cue stick. Ridley had been semihard since Alex had walked into the pub, but when he bent over the table to line up his shot, Ridley's jeans got a whole lot tighter. He'd never been a big fan of the skinny-jean fad, but seeing Alex in them changed his opinion. He fucking loved the crazy fad.

Alex pulled back his arm and the muscles bulged when he broke, the cue ball connecting with a loud crack sending the balls scattering, one falling into a side pocket.

"Well look at that. I actually made one," Alex exclaimed with a smirk.

"What have you got?"

"Big ones," Alex responded and moved around the table eyeing his options. He leaned over the table and lined up the cue, but before he took the shot he looked up at Ridley and met his gaze. "And before you ask, yes, I do have big ones."

Any witty comeback he might have had was obliterated in the wake of Alex's captivating gaze in combination with the naughty images that popped into Ridley's head with Alex's declaration. He shifted slightly and swallowed down his moan as his erection rubbed against the rough front seam of his jeans.

"You're picturing it, aren't you?" Alex murmured knowingly before taking his shot.

"Yes."

Ridley was so mesmerized by Alex's movements, the way he stroked his hand down the cue stick as he studied the table, the way he shifted from foot to foot causing that amazing ass to sway and tighten, the way he bit his lower lip before taking a shot, Ridley didn't even realize Alex had run the table until he was calling out his last shot.

"Eight ball in the corner pocket," he exclaimed and pointed at the pocket in question with his cue stick.

"Hey! I thought you said you sucked at pool?" Ridley huffed.

"I said I sucked at pool when I was stone-cold sober," Alex pointed out. "After a few beers to relax me, I fucking rock," he said smugly.

True to his word, Alex smacked the cue ball and it ricocheted off the side bumper at the perfect angle and sunk the eight ball into the intended pocket.

Alex flashed a brilliant smile at Ridley and hung up his cue stick before grabbing the rack. "Best of three?"

So that's how he wanted to play. "Bring it."

Ridley held his own during the next game, which was pretty damn remarkable considering how much Alex teased him. The bastard found every excuse to brush up against him, each time flashing Ridley a naughty smile. The hardest tease to ignore, because it caused his own dick to throb each time, was the way Alex touched himself. Every time Ridley would look at him, Alex would rub a palm over the impressive bulge at the front of his jeans or across his chest. The fucker even rubbed both his hands over his ass as he ordered more beers. Ridley was going out of his goddamn head. It was impossible to concentrate on the game when all he wanted to do was rip Alex's clothes off and bend him over the pool table. To slam some balls against taut skin rather than padded tables or stroke a pole rather than a cue stick. Ridley was a fucking mess, but he won. Yeah, yeah, yeah, so Alex scratched on the eight ball, but it served him right, teasing Ridley like that.

Ridley gulped down half his beer, the cool liquid soothing his dry throat, before he moved up close to Alex and inhaled deeply. The man smelled of beer, spice, clean sweat, and a unique scent that caused Ridley's pulse to speed and his dick to throb. He wanted to touch and taste every inch of the addictive man. Emboldened by the way Alex had been teasing him all night, he whispered, "I say we call it a draw and celebrate our wins back at my place."

Alex sucked in a deep breath and pushed his ass against Ridley's groin, pulling a deep, rumbling moan from him before stepping away. "Or we could put a little wager on the last game," Alex suggested with a sly grin.

Ridley liked his idea better. With the sexual tension arcing in the air between them each time they got close or touched, he knew he was going to get laid. He didn't want to play anymore. He was ready to get down to the fucking—beyond ready. But the wicked glint in Alex's eyes had him curious. "I'll bite. What's the stakes?"

Alex grabbed his cue stick and chalked it up. He scanned the area— no one was paying them any attention. Alex stepped up close and growled, "I like biting." Ridley shivered, causing Alex to chuckle. "I win, I top. You win, you top," he offered and chomped his teeth close to Ridley's ear before moving back to the pool table.

Oh fuck me! Ridley sucked in a harsh breath as he adjusted his aching dick, not bothering to be discreet. "Deal!"

When Alex bent to take his shot, Ridley prayed he'd run the table. If he got a chance at the table he was so going after the eight ball. No fucking way was he going to win the game. Alex obviously didn't have the same idea about losing. Within two minutes every solid was knocked in and he was studying the table. One more ball and they were out of there, and Ridley's ultimate sexy dream would be coming true. Oh Jesus H. Christ, he was going to get banged. He was literally vibrating with anticipation. He tipped up his mug with a shaking hand and gulped down the last of his beer.

"Well, if it isn't nerd boy."

Ridley lowered his mug in time to see Kyle step up and slap Alex on the back—hard—just as he was taking his shot. Alex was pitched forward, and the eight ball jumped over the railing with the powerful impact of the cue.

Alex spun and shoved Kyle with both hands. "What the fuck is your problem?" he snarled as Kyle went stumbling back.

With lightning speed, Ridley was standing between the two in full-on protective mode, putting Alex behind him. Kyle righted himself quickly and took a step toward them with his hand curled into a tight fist.

"Take one more step, motherfucker, and you'll be spitting out teeth," Ridley promised.

"Ridley," Alex barked from behind him and grabbed on to his shirt. "I can handle this."

Ridley stood his ground, reaching behind him to grab on to Alex's hip and shove him back. "I got this," Ridley growled lowly without breaking eye contact with Kyle, daring him.

"Oh, what? You got your faggot boyfriend protecting you now, nerd boy?" Kyle spat in disgust, but not until a couple of his jock buddies stepped up on either side of him.

Asswipe wouldn't have had the balls to say it without backup. Kyle didn't intimidate him. In fact, Ridley adjusted his grip on the cue stick, preparing to swing it like a Louisville Slugger if any of them made the slightest advance.

"We're not having any of this shit in my place," Jake snapped, boldly stepping in between the group of posturing and pissed-off men. He'd obviously witnessed what had taken place because he pointed a finger at Kyle. "Take it someplace else."

With a murderous gaze, Kyle looked at Ridley for a moment longer and then threw one at Jake. "I'm going," he grunted. He turned to Ridley and said, "This ain't over." He nodded toward the door and stomped away, Tweedle Dumb and Tweedle Dumber right on his heels.

"Name the place and time," Ridley yelled out and then was shoved forward. Still surging with anger, he spun around and glared at Alex.

"Well aren't you just sexy as fuck when you're all riled up," Alex laughed. "Don't be so upset, you won the game."

Alex's words took him aback and he tilted his head in confusion. Then it hit him. "Dammit! Another reason to hate that son of a bitch," Ridley grumbled. "Best of five?"

Alex laughed harder, handed Ridley his coat, and slung an arm around his shoulders and led him toward the door. "Since the awkward conversation of preference has been averted, the only question now is your place or mine?"

"That's easy." He slid his arm around Alex's waist. "Whichever is closer."

CHAPTER 3

S<small>URPRISINGLY</small>, K<small>YLE</small> wasn't anywhere to be found when they stepped out of Jake's. Then again, Ridley wasn't sure why he was shocked. Kyle wasn't the kind of guy who threw down when the odds weren't in his favor. What should have amazed him was that Kyle tried to start shit with Alex with Ridley there in the first place. The only reason he could think of was perhaps Kyle didn't think he'd step up to defend Alex once he'd seen the two big goons Kyle had with him. Dickhead had assumed wrong, and Ridley was sure he hadn't heard the last of Kyle. He'd be wise to watch his back. He wasn't really worrying about it, though, as he unlocked the door to his small studio apartment and ushered Alex in.

The apartment was small, like really fucking tiny. Think dorm room with a private bathroom. But it had a queen-size bed with clean sheets. It was all they needed at the moment. Ridley grabbed Alex, spun him around, and shoved him up against the closed door.

"I've wanted to do this all night," he growled before smashing their mouths together. He moaned loudly as his tongue passed Alex's lips and Ridley got the first taste of Alex's delicious warm, wet mouth.

Apparently Alex had wanted the same thing. He may have been the one pinned against the door, but he was far from passive. Alex grabbed Ridley's face in both his hands as he tried to take control of the kiss. It was hard and fast, all swirling tongues, clanking teeth, and working lips. Ridley gave as good as he got, but Alex directed it, controlled it until Ridley could do nothing but react.

He wasn't complaining that Alex had won the battle. There were other places on the sexy man he could have his way with while Alex continued to devour Ridley's mouth. They were the same height and their groins fit perfectly together. Ridley's hands trembled slightly as he moved them down Alex's chest. There was nothing geekish or weak about Alex's body. It was all hard lines and taut muscle. The ridges on his flat stomach flexed beneath Ridley's fingers. Alex was much more powerful and muscled than Ridley had originally thought. He was curious as to how a bookworm had built up such an impressive body. Ridley was a regular at the campus gym, and he'd never seen Alex there. He'd have to ask him, but not right then. Not while he was stroking his palm over Alex's hardness. Ridley didn't care how Alex had gotten so much muscle. He only wanted to touch, taste, pinch—*mmm*—and bite.

Alex broke the kiss and grabbed Ridley's wrist as he tried to pop the button on Alex's jeans. "Not so fast," Alex murmured.

"Why the hell not?" Ridley grunted impatiently, wanting to get his hands on the goods, and fast. The words were barely out of his mouth when he was spun around and his back hit the door so hard a loud "oomph" escaped him.

"What's the matter, tough boy?" Alex said slyly. "I'd have thought you liked it rough."

Ridley clutched Alex's hips and pulled him forward hard. They both hissed when their groins came in contact. "Oh, I like it rough, all right," he assured him. "But I figured I'd have to go easy on you."

Alex licked his swollen bottom lip and then smirked. "That would be your first mistake," he drawled.

The wicked glint in his eyes caused Ridley's body to thrum and a thrill to race down his spine. The sensation intensified when Alex fisted his hands in Ridley's dress shirt and yanked, the buttons making small pings as they hit the wood floor.

Ridley opened his mouth to protest the rough treatment of his good shirt, but he couldn't. Not when Alex leaned down and sucked Ridley's right nipple into his mouth, teeth scraping against the sensitive nub. He couldn't give a shit about clothes right then. Alex could have shredded them, and Ridley wouldn't have given a fuck in that moment.

Fingers curling in the silky strands at the back of Alex's head, Ridley pressed Alex's face harder against his chest. Alex grunted and then bit down hard enough Ridley felt it all the way down to his cock. He looked down and shuddered at the sight of Alex's mouth on him. Alex's dark lips and pink tongue looked good against Ridley's smooth, pale skin. Felt even better.

"Hands at your sides," Alex demanded he moved over to the other nip.

Alex bit down on the erect nub and pinched the first nipple at the same time, causing Ridley to gasp. He didn't know why he was so surprised by Alex's aggressive behavior, since Alex had been hinting at it all night. To actually experience it, though, was a major turn-on, as was the dual sensation of pleasure and pain.

Ridley cried out when the pleasure gave way to more pain. "Hands at your sides," Alex repeated, the tone of his voice like the crack of a whip. Ridley instantly lowered his hands.

"Jesus, you're a pushy fucker."

Alex got right in Ridley's face, their noses practically touching. Both of Alex's hands went to Ridley's nipples, pinching, tugging them sharply, and then rolling them in his fingers. "You got a problem with pushy?" Alex challenged.

Jaw clenched tightly as he tried to process the pain from Alex assaulting his nipples, Ridley didn't dare speak. Instead he shook his head.

"You got a problem with me being a fucker?" Alex then asked slyly as he continued his torturous treatment.

Again Ridley shook his head.

Alex pressed a quick kiss to his lips and then nipped at the bottom one before he said, "Good."

Alex went back to using his mouth on Ridley's nipples, only this time he licked and kissed each abused nub, soothing the sting with soft lips and swirling tongue. It felt good, but Ridley was already missing the sharper edge of teeth and fingers. The sting wasn't the only thing he was missing when Alex took a step back, depriving Ridley of his mouth and heat.

"Take your clothes off."

Ridley was so turned on he didn't even question it, simply followed Alex's command. Alex watched intently, his blue eyes dark with lust, as Ridley let his jeans and briefs fall to the floor and then stepped out of them. Standing there completely naked, his cock hard and curling upward, Ridley preened a little, enjoying the appreciative look on Alex's face. Ridley wrapped a fist around his cock, stroking the entire length slowly.

"That's mine," Alex growled and slapped Ridley's hand away.

Ridley had always fancied himself an aggressive lover, taking what he wanted when he wanted. He preferred to bottom but was a total fucking power bottom, knowing what he liked, how he liked it, and not afraid to take it. He wasn't used to being told what to do, but with Alex calling the shots, he loved it.

He couldn't help but taunt Alex a bit, however. "Yeah? What you going to do with it?" he asked, wiggling his hips, his dick bobbing and swaying obscenely.

Ridley's cockiness fled when Alex answered his question by dropping to his knees and swallowing Ridley down, greedily sucking and licking. Ridley gasped and then grabbed a handful of Alex's curls and thrust hard into that warm, willing mouth.

Alex jerked back. "Hands at your sides."

"What the fuck, man?" Ridley panted and thrust his cock at him. "What is it with you and my hands? I'm really good with them," he said confidently.

"I'm sure you are, and you can prove your boast later." Alex grinned wickedly and arched a brow at Ridley. "Now put them at your fucking sides and don't touch me if you want me to suck your dick."

Who in the hell was Ridley to argue? His dick was weeping, balls aching, so of course his hands were at his sides in record time. Ridley had to curl them into tight fists because the urge to touch Alex was huge, but the desire to have Alex bobbing and slurping on his pole was even greater.

Alex pinned Ridley's hips against the door, his grip and strength enough to ensure Ridley couldn't move at all while Alex took Ridley back into his mouth and swallowed him down. It was both the most pleasurable thing he'd ever experienced as well as the most frustrating. He watched Alex hungrily feast on his dick, the constriction of his throat the perfect friction each time he swallowed and the noises he was making causing vibrations all the way to Ridley's toes. He was in fucking heaven. Yet not being able to move, unable to touch, was pure hell.

"You're driving me insane," Ridley moaned.

Alex pulled off Ridley's dick with a pop and smirked up at him. "Well, let me help you get there faster," he said huskily.

And Jesus, Joseph, and Mary, he was speeding right toward crazy when Alex took him in to the hilt, at the same time shoving the tip of one dry finger up Ridley's ass. "Fuck!" he shouted at the burn as Alex worked the finger deeper.

Ridley pounded on the door with his fists, trying to hump for all he was worth and bearing down on Alex's finger. It was raw and dirty and he felt like a total fucking slut, a slut who was about to blow his load.

"Close," Ridley gritted out between clenched teeth.

The first time Ridley was with a guy, he hoped he swallowed; it was something that always got him off hard. However, Ridley was hoping Alex didn't, because he couldn't think of anything hotter than watching Alex's gorgeous face as he came all over it.

"Come for me," Alex growled as he wrapped a tight fist around Ridley's cock.

It only took one hard pull on his dick while Alex continued to fuck Ridley's ass with his finger and Ridley was shouting out his release. His eyes threatened to close at the intensity of his orgasm racing down his spine, but there was no way he was going to miss a second of seeing Alex take his load. And yes, Alex was beyond fucking perfect, or maybe he could read Ridley's naughty thoughts, because Alex opened his mouth wide and pumped him hard and fast. The first blast landed on Alex's cheek, but he adjusted his aim and the rest landed on his tongue.

Between the look of pleasure on Alex's face as he looked up with heavy-lidded eyes and the perfect friction on his dick, Ridley came harder and longer than he ever had before, babbling, cursing, and shouting until Alex had milked every last drop.

Ridley slumped against the wall, legs shaking so hard they threatened to give out, but Alex wasn't done yet. Instead of giving Ridley a minute to catch his breath, Alex crooked his finger, pressing it hard against Ridley's prostate, and took his dick back into his mouth. He was relentless, sucking hard, cum dripping from the corners of his lips. It was hot as hell, Alex on his knees, fully clothed, sucking and slurping, but Jesus, Ridley's cock was overly sensitive after just having come. He struggled between wanting to continue watching the sexy fucker enjoying his knob and wanting him to stop. His body made the choice for him, and he fisted his hand in Alex's curls and tried to pull him off. Alex refused to be moved or stop.

"Enough," Ridley begged, squirming and pulling at Alex's hair.

Alex's hands tightened on Ridley's hips and he ignored the plea. Instead, he sucked harder on Ridley's—to his surprise—still-hard cock.

"Dammit, Alex, enough!" he shouted.

Ridley hissed when the finger in his ass disappeared, but sighed when Alex sat back on his calves.

"Pansyass," Alex snorted as he wiped the back of his hand across his mouth.

Ridley closed his eyes and rested his head against the door. "Give me a minute and I'll show you just how pansy I am not," he gruffed.

Alex began to laugh. Ridley didn't know what, but something in the tone or maybe it was the smug look on his face had Ridley vibrating. Whatever it was, he was on Alex in a flash and they were rolling around on the floor. He pawed at Alex's clothes. Alex dug his fingers into Ridley's bare flesh, both trying to get the upper hand. They crashed into furniture, upending a side table and sending the lamp crashing to the floor, the bulb shattering.

Ridley got Alex's shirt off and briefly got control of him, straddling his lean hips. "You're a tough little fucker," Ridley said wryly. Being smug around Alex wasn't the best of choices. It ramped him up. It was evident in his blue eyes. They'd gotten darker, and he narrowed them as if he were surprised Ridley had had the balls to challenge him. He liked to challenge Alex. He wanted to see just how far he could push him and how far Alex would take him up on a taunt. When Alex tried to roll him, Ridley anticipated the move and tried to go with it, get enough momentum that they'd continue to roll until he was once again on top. However, his place was small, too much furniture and clutter, and Ridley ended up on his back, smashed against a bookcase with Alex leering down at him.

"I'm tough," Alex said assuredly and popped the button on his jeans. "And right now I'm going to be the toughest fucker you've ever met when I'm shoving my dick up your ass."

And damn if he didn't.

Alex had him on the bed, laid out on his back, in minutes. Holy shit, Ridley wasn't complaining. Alex had a nice long, fat cock, like nine inches and fucking thick. All Ridley could do was lie there, drooling and thrumming with anticipation and honestly a little worried, while Alex rolled on a condom. Ridley was no virgin, far from it. But it had been a while and Alex's dick was impressive as hell. Ridley knew it was going to hurt, but he was ready for the challenge.

Only Alex made him wait.

Alex kneeled at the foot of the bed, taking his dear sweet time with lubing up his fingers. He kept his gaze on Ridley the whole time, alternating between his eyes and his dick. Ridley couldn't tell what Alex was thinking, his expression too neutral. Ridley was sure he looked wanton with his legs spread wide, his dick straining and weeping, but he didn't fucking care. In fact, he was moaning, although he didn't really know why since Alex wasn't touching him. Frustration maybe? Ridley knew not to say anything; this was Alex's game and Ridley was eager to play along. But damn if he didn't wish Alex would hurry the fuck up.

Alex tossed the lube aside and rubbed his hands together. "Put a pillow beneath your ass and open yourself up."

Ridley hesitated. He'd never been one to follow orders blindly, so this was a whole new experience for him, albeit a hot one. But it only took a hard glare from Alex and Ridley was doing as he was told. He grabbed his ass cheeks and spread them wide, legs in the air like a total whore.

Alex pushed a single finger into Ridley's ass. He gave no warning, just shoved it deep, and Ridley grunted with the burn. He'd had a dry finger in his ass before and he'd been okay with it, but Christ, he wasn't expecting Alex to shove it to the hilt and start fucking him hard and fast without giving him time to adjust. Alex held his gaze, seeming to enjoy watching Ridley struggle. Ridley had to admit, he kind of liked it too.

"Can you take another one?"

Ridley wasn't sure if he could, at least not right at that moment, but he wanted Alex's dick so fucking bad he was willing to suffer a little to get it sooner. "Only one way to find out."

The second finger hurt, but again it was more burn than actual pain. What caused his heart to pound hard was the way Alex's eyes smoldered as he watched his fingers going in and out of Ridley's ass. He cried out when Alex shoved those thick fingers in hard and deep, but Alex didn't let that stop him. Nope, he fucked Ridley's ass even harder until he was grunting and panting and squirming like a fucking madman. Alex obviously was paying more attention to the way Ridley's cock was as hard as a rock and leaking than to his cries. Alex was right. Ridley liked the edge of pain.

"Damn, you're hot," Alex murmured. He leaned in and bit the inside of Ridley's thigh.

Ridley tried to say thank you, but it came out as a guttural moan as Alex bit and sucked hard on Ridley's sensitive flesh. He was going to be bruised in the morning and damn his ass was going to be sore, but he didn't care. Ridley bucked against the pain, bore down on those turning and twisting fingers in his ass. Alex played with Ridley's ass, completely focused on it. One finger, then two, alternating hands, a thumb, twisting them, hooking his fingers and stabbing at Ridley's prostate, which made him cry out each and every time. He didn't even care when Alex added a third. He was so turned on and Alex was practically punching his fingers into him, but holy fuck, the look on Alex's face was so hot Ridley would have let him shove his whole goddamn arm up there as long as he kept looking at him like that, consequences be damned.

Thankfully he didn't try more than three because Ridley would have paid for it later. Instead, Alex pulled his fingers out and slapped Ridley hard on the ass. "Roll over, head down, ass up, and grab on to the headboard."

Ridley rolled instantly into the position Alex directed and waited. Alex didn't move, didn't make a sound, but Ridley could feel Alex's eyes boring into him. He was moaning and humping the air and begging with his body. God, how he wanted Alex to shove his fat cock deep inside him, wanted to feel the sensation of being split wide open. The thought made him whimper and hump harder. But Alex didn't play by the rules. He took the opportunity the new position allowed and played with Ridley's ass some more. He slapped it, which made Ridley cry out because it fucking stung, but he also pushed back against Alex's hand, silently demanding more. Alex gave it. He beat Ridley's ass, kneaded it, poked it, even bent down and bit it.

Ridley screamed when Alex's teeth sunk in. "You are one sadistic fucker."

Alex's response was to laugh and do it again. He didn't break the skin, but Jesus fuck, Ridley was going to be bruised and marked and more than likely wouldn't be able to sit down come morning. Ridley would worry about that when he woke. For now he was riding the edge of pleasure and pain and what a fucking rush it was.

Alex tortured and pleasured Ridley until the pain began to overwhelm him. He tightened his hold on the headboard till his knuckles were white and tears threatened. It was on the tip of his tongue to tell Alex to back the fuck off. Alex must have known it too, because suddenly there was a wet tongue licking along his crease. The gentle swipes of Alex's tongue made him sigh and let him unclench his jaw. Then Alex pushed his tongue in, which felt like a fucking dream in Ridley's raw ass. Alex dug his fingers into the meaty flesh of Ridley's ass cheeks, pulled them apart, and buried his face, fucking Ridley hard with his tongue. So much for the reprieve on his jaw. He was once again clenching it, but this time because he was on the verge of coming. Amazing since Alex hadn't even touched Ridley's dick. Again, Alex read him like an open book, and just as Ridley was about to blow, he backed off, denied Ridley his tongue and fingers. Ridley groaned both in relief and frustration.

"I'm going to fuck you now," Alex growled. "I'm going to fuck you so hard you'll see stars."

"Yes please," Ridley moaned. Or at least that's what he thought he'd said or tried to say, but he wasn't sure if what came out could be distinguished as human speech, because Alex was shoving his fat sheathed cock into him at the same time he voiced the warning. Ridley sounded more like a fucking animal than human, and then Alex fucked him like one.

It was one of the roughest fucks Ridley had ever experienced. He'd completely misjudged Alex. He was very powerful. The grip he had on Ridley's hips was like a vise, and not only did Alex plow into him with brute strength, he pulled Ridley back onto that thick cock at the same time. Alex was so fucking deep inside him with each thrust, Ridley could have sworn he was choking on Alex's cock.

It took a bit, but Ridley found his rhythm and started rocking, clenching his ass, trying to keep Alex inside him. Alex had other plans. He pulled all the way out, wait for Ridley's asshole to contract, and then he'd slam into him again.

"That's it," Alex hissed. "Fuck yourself on my cock. Show me what a little slut you are."

Ridley did. He felt dirty and nasty and didn't care. He held on to the bed to keep from being shoved through it and used it as leverage to slam his ass back with each thrust. He was sweating and cussing; the headboard was slamming into the wall, and he swore the goddamn room was shaking. It wouldn't have surprised him one bit if Alex fucked him not only through the mattress, but right through the motherfucking floor. Still, when Alex shuddered and came inside him, his shout was so loud Ridley's ears rang. He wished Alex hadn't had the condom on because the only thing that would have made it more perfect would have been to feel Alex's hot spunk filling him, then running down his legs.

For a few minutes Alex lay across Ridley's back, breathing hard, his face buried in the back of Ridley's neck. His warm breath felt good, made Ridley shudder. Ridley was still hard, still aching, but he liked having Alex's weight on him. He liked the fact that Alex was breathing hard and needed a minute to compose himself after fucking him.

Once Alex calmed down and his breathing returned to normal, he nipped at the back of Ridley's neck and then said, "Roll over."

Ridley lay back on the pillow. Alex wrapped his fist around Ridley's cock and held his gaze as he jerked him off. Alex didn't play with Ridley's ass this time, which was fine because it fucking hurt, but Alex rolled his balls roughly in his other hand while he tugged on Ridley. Alex's rhythm was hard and fast as he pumped his cock, fire shining in Alex's blue eyes, and Ridley knew Alex liked what he saw. He started to stroke harder and harder, tightening his fist till it nearly hurt. Ridley wanted to come so bad his balls were aching, and he was clamping down so hard on his teeth he thought they would shatter.

Alex's hair was damp, sweat rolling down his face and chest. His softening cock swayed with each movement. And those eyes. Christ the man was so fucking sexy and as impossibly hard as it was to hold on, Ridley didn't want the moment to end.

But then Alex whispered, "Come."

Ridley did and holy hell, it was huge. He'd thought he'd come hard when Alex had sucked him off, but this was beyond huge, and Ridley really did see stars like Alex had promised. Alex worked him until he'd pulled every last drop out of him. Ridley closed his eyes and melted into the mattress. He felt Alex leave the bed, but he didn't know what Alex was doing, too spent to move. His entire body felt like a limp noodle and even his dick had had enough. Ridley pulled the covers up over his head and that was it for his strength.

It surprised Ridley when Alex didn't bolt; instead, he slid under the covers and snuggled up to Ridley's side. Alex was a cuddler and Ridley liked that shit.

He wrapped an arm around Alex, completely sated, enjoying the afterglow and Alex's warmth. Ridley would have sworn not even a nuke could have made him move, but loud banging on the door followed by "Police! Open the door!" had him jumping out of bed.

"Fuck! What the hell do they want?" Ridley growled and snatched up the throw blanket that had ended up halfway beneath his bed. He wrapped it around his waist and swayed on shaky legs to the door. Hand on the knob, Ridley looked back over his shoulder and saw Alex wasn't going to be any help. He had pulled the covers up over his head, hiding. Fucker.

Ridley looked out the peephole to make sure it wasn't one of the assholes in the building that liked to pull pranks. But it really was the cops, and he opened the door a crack.

"Can I help you?" Ridley's voice came out like a rasp, his throat raw from screaming.

"Good evening, sir. We've gotten a complaint about the noise. Everything okay?"

"Uh, um, yeah," Ridley stuttered. "Sorry about the noise we were just umm… you know." He shrugged.

"The caller said there was fighting going on. Is there anyone here with you, sir?"

"Yes. But we weren't fighting."

The one officer looked at the other; both had their hands close to their guns. *What the hell*? He just wanted to go lay his sore ass down, snuggle, and relax. Instead, he had the fucking cops ready to draw their weapons. Jesus!

"I'm going to need you to open the door, sir."

"For what?" Ridley asked. "I just said we weren't fighting. If you must know we were fucking." He didn't even trying to hide his irritation.

The big officer with Franks imprinted on his badge arched a brow, but he didn't move his hand away from his gun. "Sir, I'm going to have to insist that you open the door."

"Fine!" Ridley threw open the door but didn't move out of the way to allow them entrance. They could see the lump in his bed easily from the door. "See—we were fucking and we're done so I'll be sure to keep the noise down."

"Ma'am, are you okay?" Franks asked, pushing his way past Ridley.

Alex didn't take the covers from his face, but he did sneak an arm out and hold a thumb up. "I'm good," he snickered, his voice low and scratchy and so not that of a chick.

The one officer who hadn't said a word coughed, and Ridley caught him covering his mouth, trying not to laugh. The other one's eyes got so big Ridley thought they were going to pop out of his head, and he took a step back.

"Oh…. Alrighty, then," he stammered. "Just keep it down and…." He shook his head. "Please don't make me come back here tonight." He stormed off down the hall without looking back.

The smaller officer—Ridley didn't get a look at his badge—winked at him and gave a thumbs-up before he followed his partner.

Ridley shut the door and Alex just started fucking howling. He grabbed onto his gut as he laughed his damn fool head off. Ridley couldn't help but laugh right along with him. Officer Franks's expression when he realized the *ma'am* was actually a *sir* had been priceless. Plus it had been a first. Being fucked so hard the cops had to come and check on him was fucking epic. The thought made Ridley laugh even harder.

Ridley joined Alex under the covers and pulled him close. "I scream, you scream, the police come. It's awkward," Ridley recited from a post he'd seen on his Twitter. It was totally appropriate.

Alex hooted again, shook the whole damn bed with it. Ridley was pretty sure Alex was still laughing when he drifted off. It *was* pretty fucking hilarious.

CHAPTER 4

BEING A light sleeper, Ridley was surprised to find himself alone the next morning. Obviously he'd been out cold. He had neither heard nor felt Alex leave the bed, but when Ridley looked around the room, it was only his own clothes on the floor. Ridley rubbed at his eyes and started to sit up but yelped and slumped back down on the mattress when his ass reminded him with searing pain that it wasn't a good idea just yet.

Ridley cautiously moved his fingers and toes, working his way around his body, taking in a damage assessment. His legs were a little sore, hips a little more so, but it was his chest, the area around the nipples, that had him a little concerned. He shoved the covers down and gasped. His chest was covered with dark hickeys and teeth marks. There was a deep purple spot above his belly button and some wicked bruises on his hips. His dick was coated with a nasty crust of dried cum and looked a lot smaller than it normally did in the morning, almost like it was trying to hide inside for fear Ridley might actually want to use it again. But it was his ass that had taken the brunt of Alex's aggression. He'd be feeling Alex for days.

It took a while—along with lots of groaning, cursing and wincing—but he finally made it to the shower. As he washed his sore and aching body—there might have been tears in his eyes when he washed his dick and ass—Ridley was glad Alex had snuck out. He wasn't sure how he would have handled Alex seeing him crying like a little sissy. Okay that was probably a little dramatic, but it did really fucking hurt.

He used exceptional care when drying off and knew there was no way he could handle wearing jeans, so instead he slipped into a pair of old, worn sweats and took in the wreck of a room. He wasn't about to clean it up, not with the throbbing pain in his ass and chest, but he did smirk while his coffee brewed as he remembered how the room had ended up looking like a tornado had touched down in the center of it. A tornado by the name of Alex Firestone.

It took a couple days to actually do more than lounge around and watch TV, but slowly the ass-tearing pain gave way to a nice dull ache, and the glutton for punishment he was, he found himself wanting a repeat performance. But Alex hadn't bothered to come by and worse, he hadn't responded to Ridley's text messages.

Ridley wasn't a cling-on and he hadn't been expecting flowers or any such shit, but he was slightly irritated that Alex couldn't be bothered to reply to a simple text of "hello." Funny, Ridley was usually the one who didn't call back or return messages. He didn't like complications and understood fucking was fucking. However, Alex was different, no matter how much Ridley tried to convince himself otherwise. Logically, he knew they had both gotten what they wanted—to get laid. *The best damn lay you've ever had.*

Ridley snatched his phone from the nightstand and checked it for the twentieth time since he'd gotten up. Fuck, he was turning into such a schoolgirl, a fact driven home when his chest tightened and his gut rolled in disappointment.

"Ugh!" He flopped down on the bed and ran his hands through his hair. Obviously his thick skull wasn't getting the message—the guy wanted nothing more to do with him. Ridley needed to get out of the apartment before he drove himself nuts.

He slipped on his jeans, T-shirt, and tennis shoes and headed out. He planned on going downtown to Jake's for a beer and a burger, but when he stopped, he found himself standing outside the library. *Dammit!* Ridley shoved his hands into the front pockets of his jeans and started pacing back and forth, the song lyrics "Should I stay or should I go?" playing on a continuous loop in his head. "Yup, total fucking schoolgirl," he growled under his breath and bounded up the steps.

Ridley briefly wondered what people saw on his face when he pushed through the doors, because he was pretty sure he looked like a madman as he scanned the area and couldn't find Alex. And that had nothing on how he must have looked when he repeated the scene the next day, and the next.

He was beginning to get worried. He'd been coming to the library since the fall semester had begun, and Alex always worked on Tuesdays and Wednesdays. He spotted Amanda and rushed over. "Hey, Amanda. Remember me?" he asked, trying hard not to scare her with his craziness.

"Oh, hi," she said with a wave. "Sorry, I don't think I caught your name."

"Ridley." He held out his hand.

"Nice to officially meet you, Ridley." She shook his hand and smiled. "What can I do for you?"

"Is Alex working today?"

"Nope."

He waited for her to elaborate but she only shrugged. "Is he going to be here tomorrow?" he pressed.

"Nope, won't be here the rest of the week."

The unease intensified. "Is he sick?"

"Don't know."

Alrighty, then. He wanted to drill Amanda for more, but it was obvious from her curt answers and the way she was beginning to look at him suspiciously that he wasn't going to get more out of her. He should have let it drop there, left well enough alone. It was beginning to become pretty apparent the bastard was avoiding him. Unfortunately it was easier said than done, because he simply couldn't get Alex out of his head and something in his gut kept gnawing at him.

"I THINK I'm losing my damn mind," Ridley said by way of greeting when Rae slid into the booth at Jake's.

"Sorry, hun, but that happened years ago," she chuckled and grabbed his beer, taking a big gulp.

"Well aren't you just fucking hilarious," he grumbled as he snatched his mug from her and downed the last of the lukewarm brew.

"That's why you love me," Rae said confidently and waved over the waiter.

Ridley ordered them each a beer and paid for them. It sucked that he had to bribe his best friend into coming out with free booze. In her defense, she did have an exam early the next morning, but he was desperate.

"Remember that guy I went out with the other night?"

"The hot geek? Yeah, what about him?"

"I haven't heard from him since he left my apartment and he hasn't been at work."

Rae cocked her head and gave him a confused look. "And the problem is?"

"I can't find him and he's not returning my calls," Ridley complained.

"I still don't see the problem. You guys hooked up, you fucked, you went your separate ways. You've been playing the same game for years." Rae's eyes went wide. "Don't tell me you're actually falling for someone?" Her tone was full of shock.

They'd been best friends since they were in high school. She was his confidant, and there wasn't much about him she didn't know. So her incredulousness over his revelation was well founded. He'd never cared about a guy he'd fucked. Fucking was one thing and the clingy guys who expect more from Ridley had always bothered him. For the first time, he found he was "one of those guys," and to say it had him feeling a little bit of guilt for the way he'd treated guys in the past was a huge understatement. Being used for sex sucked!

"I'm just worried about him is all," he deadpanned, but he was pretty sure she could tell he was lying since he couldn't meet her eyes. The suds in his beer were way easier to look at.

"Oh. My. God!" Rae said excitedly. "Ridley Corbin actually has some feelings beneath that tough-as-nails exterior."

"I hate you," he muttered, but he couldn't help but smile. She knew him too well.

"So he's not calling you and your gut is all messed up and you can't sleep or think of anything but Alex. Oh and you're constantly checking your cell phone like you were some crazy-in-lurve high school girl, right?" she said smugly, because damn if she didn't get it right and she knew it.

"Did I mention I hate you?"

Ignoring his crass words, Rae leaned her elbows on the table and studied him. Rae was working on a degree in psychology, and Ridley could see the steam coming from her ears as she tried to figure out how to help him with his craziness. She'd always tried to get him on her therapy couch and "fix" him and his "inability to make meaningful connections with people." Ridley thought he'd made some great connections in his past. His dick connecting to a hot ass or an even better connection—a hot wet mouth connecting with his dick or a thick pole connecting with his ass. *Focus, dude.* He knew what she meant now that he'd met Alex.

"So, for the first time, you're actually considering foregoing the one-night stand and thinking of the scary second date, huh?"

Ridley gritted his teeth and leered at her, but she only smiled and waited. He was caught and knew it, so he just sighed and nodded his head.

"And you want this second date with Alex Firestone."

Nod.

"And he's avoiding you," she reiterated.

Nod. Nod. Nod.

Rae was silent for a long moment. When the silence stretched out way too long for comfort, Ridley gave her a questioning look. "Well?"

"You're going to have to admit to him your intentions."

"I did. I texted him," Ridley said defensively. "Isn't that admission enough?"

"Nope."

"What do you mean *nope*?" Between Rae and Amanda, the word was beginning to grate on his damn nerves.

Rae waved a hand dismissively. "I know you. I'm sure your text consisted of *hey* or *what up?* or some other stupid macho crap." She pointed a finger at him. "You need to tell him you want to see him. Ask him out on a date."

"No fucking way. I'm not doing that," he said adamantly and shook his head. "He's avoiding me. I'll look like a pathetic desperate loser."

"You *are* desperate and pathetic," she sniffed. "I mean, look at you. When's the last time you slept? You look like shit."

Ridley looked down at himself and then ran a hand over the week of growth on his chin. Grudgingly, he had to admit he was both of those things, but dammit, he wasn't going to tell her she was right. Instead he said, "Yeah? At least I'm not a complete loser."

"Mmmhmm."

Well, when it came to second dates, he was a loser. He'd never had one. He had no idea how to go about getting someone to go out on an actual date. He normally asked someone out with the intentions of fucking and sucking and not really caring if they even talked. He'd done that. Seduced a guy in a bar with only his eyes and was able to get his pants down and bent over the bathroom sink without ever saying a word. That had been hot as fuck, but still not as exciting as what Alex could do to him.

"Order us another beer and I'll teach you everything you'll need to know," Rae offered.

By the time he and Rae parted ways an hour later, he had a game plan. He didn't know how smart she was about relationships—she seemed to be in love at least once a month—but they'd already established he was desperate, so he was willing to try her silly Dr. Girly stuff.

After leaving the bar, Ridley was walking past the lecture hall, flipping his phone in his hand and trying to figure out how best to put Rae's words into a text with a little bit of his own style. Kyle's voice coming from down the alley between the lecture hall and the administration building turned the blood in his veins to ice.

CHAPTER 5

THE FOOTFALLS of his pursuers were getting closer. Alex scanned the area. *Too many people.* He lengthened his strides. He knew who was after him.

At first, Alex had tried to ignore Kyle. When that didn't work, he'd hoped that by showing the asshole he wasn't intimidated—which he wasn't—Kyle would look for easier prey to pick on. No such luck. Apparently Kyle had a hard-on for him and was looking for some action. He was going to have to deal with Kyle once and for all, but not here. Not with witnesses. Just past the lecture hall, Alex slipped down an alleyway, rushed to the end, and turned to face him head-on.

It wasn't the ideal place, too great a chance someone would come along, but it would have to do. Best-case scenario, he could show Kyle the error of his ways quickly and quietly, but he wasn't holding out much hope. He was even less convinced it would end peacefully. He rolled his neck, squared his shoulders, and watched intently as Kyle and his friends approached.

"I've been looking for you, nerd boy," Kyle snarled.

"Well, you found me. But I'd suggest you and your friends turn around and head back the way you came before it's too late," Alex warned, trying to keep his irritation in check, but it was difficult.

Alex just wanted to keep his head down, take his classes, and chill. The last thing he wanted was attention. Attention was dangerous. Attention could get him killed.

The five men stepped into the glow of the low light from above the steel door, Kyle leading the way, his henchmen flanking him with wide grins on their faces. A little more of Alex's control slipped away, and he briefly thought of pulling the gun he had strapped to his side. Nope, too much noise. But…. *No.* He took a deep breath and curled his hands into fists.

"You have no idea who the hell you're fucking with," Alex snarled.

"You're a brave little shit, I'll give you that," Kyle jeered. "I'm going to enjoy teaching you some manners on how to respect your betters."

"My betters?" Alex laughed. "You have got to be fucking kidding me. Dumb fuck one here," he said, pointing to John Nash, the defensive tackle on the college team and as big as fucking refrigerator, "is the only one who might give me a challenge, but even that is iffy since my guess is no muscle, all fat beneath that jacket."

"Why you little—"

Alex tensed, moving into a defensive stance, fists up.

"John, no!" Kyle snarled and shoved him aside before John could pounce. "Not yet. This little nerd boy is mine."

Kyle swung. Alex anticipated the movement, easily dodging the punch. He grabbed Kyle's shoulder, and using his own momentum against him, pulled him closer and jammed his knee into Kyle's gut, at the same time shoving him backward against his friends. One of them dropped a metal pipe, which Alex snatched up with lightning speed.

John made a move. "Batter up," Alex shouted gleefully and pulled the pipe back, readying his swing.

Ridley appeared out of nowhere, his foot connecting solidly with the side of John's knee. The howl that came out of that big fucker was proof Ridley had done some serious damage.

Son of a bitch. Where had he come from? Alex didn't have time to worry about it. Kyle and the other guys were back on their feet. *Shit, shit, shit.*

Luckily, John went flying, and Ridley toppled down with the big oaf, landing on his side. Alex heard the loud harrumph as the air rushed out of Ridley when John's shoulder connected squarely in the center of his chest. Alex would leave the two to roll around. One on one, Ridley should be safe, considering he'd already put a hurt on John and had the advantage.

Alex spun, tightened his grip on the pipe, and swung, taking out Kyle's knees before he could jump out of the way. Kyle's scream of agony was satisfying. On the upswing, the pipe hit the brick wall. A jarring pain exploded in Alex's hands and shot up his arms, causing him to lose his grip on the weapon. He didn't have time to react. A fist connected with his jaw and he stumbled back, but he managed to right himself quickly.

"Oh, you little cocksucker. You're going to pay for that," Alex warned.

Alex took a second to check on Ridley—he was sucking in harsh breaths but getting to his feet. Alex realized his error in losing focus when his wrist was grabbed, he was spun, and his arm wretched upward painfully. Alex lost his balance on the uneven concrete and fell to his knees. The impact hurt like hell, but at least it forced his attacker to release him. Alex immediately rolled and jumped to his feet. Alex slammed a well-aimed right hook into the man's mouth, followed seconds later by one to his nose. The man was out cold before he hit the ground.

Alex saw the two-by-four seconds before it connected with the back of Ridley's head. Ridley instantly fell forward, his forehead connecting with a sickening crack against John's.

"Motherfucker!" Alex howled and leapt. His boot connected with the fucker's rib cage, sending him flying into the brick wall.

Alex's gut plummeted and he raced to Ridley, who hadn't moved. Both he and John were out cold but breathing. Alex breathed in harshly as he stood over Ridley; his relief was almost as great as his anger. He didn't know whether he should hug the man or kick him.

As he surveyed the aftermath, the writhing and screaming men, the blood, the unnecessary violence, Alex began to shake, his anger taking the forefront. Pissed at Kyle and his friends for being douchebags, for forcing him to fight, for making him expose himself, at the whole fucking situation. Mostly he was pissed at Ridley for getting himself hurt and making Alex worry.

Kyle was in a fetal position, clutching his knees, moaning and groaning. "Asshole! Serves you right," Alex growled and pulled out his cellphone. "Make me have to call the goddamn law. I should have hit you in the head and knocked some fucking sense into you."

"911. What is your emergency?"

"I'm going to need a pile of shit cleaned up in the alleyway between the lecture hall and Admin building," Alex told the 911 operator and then thought of kicking Kyle again. *Asshole!*

ONE MINUTE Ridley was trying to get on his feet and struggling to get air back into his lungs, the next, pain exploded across the back of his head and then all he knew was blackness.

He woke to find Alex standing over him. It took a minute of blinking rapidly to get his face to come into focus, but Ridley knew it was him. Alex was looking all concerned, and Ridley said the first thing that popped into his head. "Would you like to go out with me sometime?"

Alex's concerned expression faded away and his lip curled into a smug grin. "I think the blow to your head rattled your brain," he commented and held out his hand.

Ridley took the offered hand and allowed Alex to pull him to a sitting position but then instantly wished he'd stayed down. The world started to spin and he grabbed the back of his head as it began to throb and shoot sharp pains down his neck.

"Don't try to get up yet," Alex ordered. "The paramedics are on the way."

Ridley didn't feel any blood, nothing damp at the back of his head, but he did have one hell of a goose egg. "Anyone get the license of the truck that hit me?"

"No, but if we roll it over we might get it," Alex said and nodded to one of the jocks laid out flat, arms stretched out liked he was flying and one hell of a shiner beneath his eye and blood running down from his split lip.

"Your work?" Ridley asked, still rubbing his head. Maybe Alex was right and the blow to his head had scattered his brains or maybe he was still out cold and dreaming, because the scene around him made no sense. Three of the five men were rolling around screaming in agony, Kyle included, but John and Shiner Boy—Ridley didn't know his name—were out cold. The kick he'd given John didn't knock him out; in fact, he was sure he'd heard him still screaming just as the pain exploded in the back of his skull. It just made no fucking sense. Ridley may have wounded John, but Alex had taken on the other four and then put John completely out of commission.

Ridley was still pondering it when he heard sirens in the distance, getting close, fast. But not as fast as the world was spinning or as rapidly as the bile was shooting up his throat. "I think I need a doctor," he groaned just before he puked all over himself.

CHAPTER 6

HE HAD a hell of a lump on the back of his head. Ridley supposed he should have been happy the fucker went for his noggin; he'd always been hardheaded. Concussion, the doc had called it, which had explained the puking—embarrassing as hell—and the ride to the hospital was pretty much a blur. One minute he was knocking John on his ass, the next thing he was in the emergency room sitting on a stretcher wearing a dress. He had flashes. He thought he remembered seeing Alex standing over him, or maybe that had been a dream, wishful thinking?

"Mr. Corbin?"

"Huh?" Ridley snapped his eyes open and scanned his surroundings. He was in a hospital room—*how the hell did I get here? Wasn't I just in the emergency room?* He was hooked up to monitors, an IV running into his arm. *What the hell?*

"Do you know what day it is?" the nurse asked and shined a light in his eyes, making him wince.

"No."

"Can you tell me your name?" she asked in a professional tone as she shined the light in his other eye.

"Attila the Hun."

"Ridley!" Rae chastised and slapped his arm.

"Ow! Stop that. I'm injured," he snapped. His head lolled to the side and he glared at Rae. "Where the hell did you come from?"

"Sir, could you please tell me your name," the nurse asked again. The old fart didn't sound at all amused.

"Ridley Corbin. Can I go home now?"

"That will be up to the doctor," Nurse Old Fart said dryly and then left the room.

Ridley sniffed and turned to Rae again, who was sitting in the chair next to the bed scowling at him. "That look doesn't work on me," he informed her. "I'm still going home."

"No, you're not," Rae said with obvious frustration. "The doctor said you had to stay overnight. You have a concussion and they need to make sure you don't die."

"That's a little dramatic, don't you think?" he asked and rolled his eyes, which made the room kind of swimmy.

"Yeah, I'd say dying is a lot dramatic, so stop being a big baby and do what the doctor tells you. He said twenty-four hours"—she pointed a finger at him—"and you're staying every last second." Ridley tried to grab the digit but his vision was blurred and he ended up with empty air, which caused Rae to laugh raucously. "Yeah, you're so ready to go home."

"I could if you would stay with me and play nurse," Ridley said hopefully, but he already knew the answer. The evil glare Rae gave him confirmed it. He wasn't going to give up, but he gave her a momentary break by changing the subject. He needed time to come up with something to guilt her with. "Hey, did you happen to see Alex?"

"Nope. I checked at the nurses' station and no one by the name Alex Firestone was brought in."

Knowing Alex hadn't come to the hospital upped Ridley's desire to get the hell out of there. His head was sketchy, the exact events elusive, and he needed to know Alex was okay. Rae had informed him that she hadn't seen Alex, and she'd arrived not too long after he had gotten to the hospital. Ridley hadn't seen him since the puking instance. The really weird thing was that the cops had thought Ridley had taken Kyle and his flunkies out. He was badass, but seriously? No.

From what little he and Rae could ascertain, the yahoos who'd started all the shit weren't talking—sudden amnesia. Probably too embarrassed to admit they tried to gang jump a single man and got their asses handed to them. Ridley also had a sneaking suspicion that the cops didn't know Alex had been there and that he wasn't supposed to talk about him. He didn't know why he thought that, but it felt right. Thinking about it made his head throb so Ridley closed his eyes. He took a few deep breaths, in through his nose and out slowly through his mouth, as the nausea returned.

"Mr. Corbin?"

"Jesus H. Christ, what now?" Ridley huffed and pulled the covers over his head.

"Sir, could you please open your eyes? I need to check your pupils," the same old fart asked and pulled the covers away.

Ridley squeezed them tighter. "Didn't we just do this?"

"Sir, that was two hours ago. Now please open your eyes."

Two hours? Holy shit! He opened his eyes and winced when the nurse shone the light in them.

"Sir, can you tell me what your name is?"

"Willy Wonka." He flinched, waiting for the slap to come. When it didn't Ridley turned his head to find the chair empty. "Do you know where my friend went?"

"She's not here."

He started to say "Thank you, Captain Fucking Obvious," but the nurse had the sense of humor of a wet noodle and pissing her off wouldn't help him with his mission to get them to release him. Instead he gritted his teeth and, trying to keep his voice as friendly as possible, asked, "Do you know how long she's been gone? Did she say where she was going?"

The nurse wrote something in her notebook, then returned it to her pocket along with her light. "She left over an hour ago, and I believe she went home," she informed him and left the room.

Fuck! He was so going to get Rae for this. How dare she leave him here alone with…. He rubbed at his burning eyes and tried to think. He needed a plan. Obviously he wasn't going to have any luck getting Rae to agree to bust him out. The doctors were refusing to release him. He guessed his only option was to go the AMA—Against Medical Advice—route. He pulled the covers back up over his head; he'd ask about the forms next time they came in.

Some time later a cute little nurse in blue scrubs and dark brown hair pulled back into a ponytail popped into his room, all smiles. "Hi, Mr. Corbin, I'm Molly and I'll be taking care of you tonight. How are you feeling?"

"Great. I'd be even better if you could bring me some AMA papers."

"You really should reconsider," Molly said cheerily. "While your X-rays and neuro check have come back normal, you still need to be monitored closely. Concussions can go from bad to worse very quickly." She hung another bag of saline and attached it to his IV pole.

"I don't think I'll be needing that," he informed her, eyeing the IV. "I'm aware of the risks. So, about those papers?"

"The doctor has ordered something for your pain. It's mild but should help take the edge off," she said, smiling broadly.

The expression on her face had him a little nervous. She looked way too happy considering he'd been a royal pain in the ass with his demands of being released. But the thought of having the vise squeezing his head eased a little was just too alluring to turn down. "Okay, sure. You can bring it at the same time you bring the papers."

Ridley knew his mistake the minute he'd swallowed the pills. Molly just laughed when he asked for the AMA papers. Apparently he wasn't of sound enough mind to make that kind of decision. She smiled broadly and winked at him just before she turned off the light and shut the door behind herself. *Sneaky bitch.*

Like the ride to the hospital, the entire night was a haze. The injury in combination with the lack of sleep was no doubt making the confusion all the more extreme. Not only was he being awakened every two hours for neuro checks, but to make matters worse, the constantly running IV fluids caused his bladder to conspire against him, keeping him up. He'd tried getting out of bed earlier on his own, but learned quickly a concussion with little sleep ended in his naked ass hitting the cold floor. No way in hell did he want to go through that again.

With a groan he rolled over and reached for the nurse's call button. He froze midmotion when he spotted a familiar blond head of curls. Alex was sitting in a chair next to Ridley's bed, elbows leaning on the mattress and head propped in his hands.

Ridley blinked several times, but the vision didn't dissipate. He tried shaking his head, but still Alex remained. "I must be dreaming," he muttered.

Alex lifted his head, looked around the sterile room, and then gave Ridley a lopsided smiled. "Not what I would call much of a dream."

Ridley shrugged. Alex was wrong. Having Alex there felt like a dream, a really good dream, and the way he smiled.... Hell yeah, it was a damn good one.

"How are you doing?" Ridley asked.

"Better than you," Alex murmured.

Ridley nodded toward Alex's swollen and bloodied knuckles. "Looks painful," he pointed out.

Alex hid his hands in his lap. "Just some scrapes. So what the hell made you jump into that mess earlier?"

"Five against one. I didn't like the odds and figured I'd help even them up a bit. Plus, I fucking hate bullies."

"I could have handled myself," Alex said with a note of pride.

"And just how in the hell is that possible? Don't get me wrong, you damn sure dominated my ass," he said dubiously. "But I kind of wanted—"

"Kind of?" Alex interrupted.

"Okay I did," Ridley muttered with a weak swat at Alex's head. "My point is, dominating my ass during sex is one thing. You taking on five assholes who want nothing more than to smash your head in is a whole other thing."

"I saved your ass," Alex said smugly.

"How?"

"Well, after the two by four came in contact with the back of your head, I took out the guy who swung it before he could hit you again." Alex's smug smile grew. "That makes *me* the one who saved *your* ass. Your hero, so to speak."

"Yeah, yeah, you're my hero," Ridley agreed. "But what I mean by 'how' is where in the hell does a library geek learn to fight like that?"

"Haven't you learned you should never judge a book by its cover? There is a lot about me you don't know, a lot of assumptions you've made based on appearance."

Alex was right. Since the moment Ridley had first laid eyes on Alex, he'd been making assumptions. After waking up covered in bruises, with aching muscles and a raw ass after a night with Alex, he should have learned his lesson. Obviously he was still making the wrong calls. However, a rough fuck still couldn't have prepared Ridley to understand how Alex could take on five muscular men, even if said muscular men were cowardly assholes.

"So clue me in. Who is Alex Firestone?"

"Mr. Corbin, it's time for your neuro check," a nurse announced as she stepped into the room and flicked on the overhead lights.

Ridley hissed and shielded his eyes with his hand. "Jesus, is it necessary to burn my damn retinas each time y'all come in here?"

"Sorry, I didn't realize you were awake," she responded, not sounding the least apologetic. "Oh," she muttered with a scowl when she noticed Alex in the chair. "You're not supposed to be here, sir. Visiting hours were over at nine."

"I called him," Ridley lied. "I... I...." He pulled at the neck of the gown. "I needed something other than a gown to wear home."

The nurse looked skeptical as she looked back and forth from him to Alex. Since there were no bags or piles of clothes, she had to know he was bullshitting her. Still, she did her checks, checking the strength in all four limbs, asking the stupid questions, and of course, doing more damage to Ridley's eyes with her penlight before leaving the room.

"I probably should get out of here before security shows up." Alex went to his feet and patted Ridley's arm. "I just wanted to check to make sure you were okay."

"Nice way to avoid the question," Ridley said wryly.

"Perhaps I'll answer it for you over a drink some time," Alex offered.

"How about you pick me up when they spring me and you can tell me about it over a decent meal?" He wrinkled his nose. "The food here sucks." Alex looked hesitant, so Ridley added, "It would help my concussed head feel better to have something to eat with my hero."

Alex didn't say anything, but based on the smile he had on his face as he headed out the door, Ridley knew he'd be seeing him over a cup of coffee or a soda. But first, bladder duty. He pushed the call button. It was his turn to bug the staff for a change.

"IN ENGLISH," Ridley said with exasperation as the doctor started rattling off discharge orders.

"Sorry," Dr. Hoffman clucked. "Your brain got slammed around inside your skull, which caused some swelling. It's going to bother you for a few days."

"Don't I know it," Ridley responded and gently rubbed at the big knot on the back of his head.

"That bump is the least of your concerns. It's what happened inside that is the problem. You'll need to take a few days off, stay quiet and no strenuous activity."

"Damn and I was hoping to get lucky," Ridley said dubiously.

Dr. Hoffman arched a brow at him but didn't comment. Instead he just shook his head before continuing. "If there is an increase in dizziness, blurring of vision, slurred speech, nausea, tremors, call an ambulance immediately. A head injury such as yours can turn ugly quickly. Do you have anyone who can stay with you for the next couple of days to watch for symptoms?"

"I'm sure I can find someone," Ridley assured him. He knew Rae probably would do it, but he was forming a plan in his head that would get him home, safe, and lucky all in one sexy geek.

"Good." Dr. Huffman handed Ridley the discharge papers. "Sign these," he instructed, giving him a pen. "I'll have the orderly take you down as soon as your ride is here."

"My ride?" he asked absently as he signed the forms.

"You can't drive until after your follow-up appointment on Friday."

"I don't live that far, I was going to walk."

"Well I guess you won't be going home today, then." Dr. Huffman shrugged. "You're staying until you have someone come get you. You better order breakfast," he said with a smirk.

"Oh hell no," Ridley protested and grabbed his cell from the bedside table.

"I thought you'd see it my way. I'll see you on Friday."

"Yeah, yeah, yeah." Bastard had him. Rae was in class until eleven and he wasn't about to sit there for the next two hours so he only had one other option.

Alex answered on the first ring. "Hello?"

"I need a hero."

"I'm your man," Alex chuckled. "What can I do for you?"

"They won't spring me unless I have someone drive me home and I—"

"I'm on my way."

Ridley sat there, stunned, as the phone went dead. He really liked the way Alex offered to come get him, just like that. It was almost as if Alex was dropping everything for him. Then again, there were a lot of feelings Alex brought out that Ridley really, really liked. Hell, the knot on the head and the sleepless night in the hospital were almost a blessing if it meant he got to spend some quality time with Alex.

By the time he pissed, got dressed in his dirty clothes, and washed his face, a nurse had come into the room pushing a wheelchair. "You ready to go?"

"I'm just waiting on my ride," he told her as he tied his shoes.

"The front desk just called to say they are here and waiting out front for you."

"Wow! That was fast. Uh, yeah, in that case I'm ready." The room tilted slightly as he stood, but luckily he didn't have far to go and flopped down into the waiting chair. A lot of guys tried to refuse a wheelchair. Ridley thought it was pretty stupid to play that macho bullshit card. He was hurt, his head was still swimming, and he was still a little nauseated. He figured going for a ride in a chair pushed by a tiny little chick was way more macho than doing a face plant on the tile floor. Hard to be manly from that position. Besides, there was no way he wanted to spend one more moment in the hospital than was absolutely necessary.

"Let's rock," he exclaimed excitedly.

The nurse gave him an exasperated look before handing him his forgotten discharge papers. "Men," she muttered and then laughed.

"Hey, I have those memorized," he grumbled.

"Uh-huh, sure you do," she said disbelievingly. "Just like you remember how you got that knot on your head."

"That was yesterday. I remember today." *Sort of.* Okay, he really didn't remember much, the knock to his noggin was messing with his short-term memory, but he remembered enough to know he was on his way to see Alex and that was all that mattered at the moment.

Outside the main entrance, he spotted Alex's car and pointed toward it. "There's my ride."

Ridley waved as Alex stepped out of the car and made his way around to the passenger side to open the door. "Thanks for coming," Ridley said sincerely as Alex helped him into the seat.

"No problem," Alex said easily.

"He tried sneaking out of here without his discharge papers," the nurse informed Alex. "I suggest you read them and keep him in line today."

"I got this," Alex told her with a wink. "I'll be sure he's a good boy."

"See that he is."

Ridley rolled his eyes.

"How are you doing?" Alex asked as he slid into the driver's seat and got them going.

"I feel like my brains are scrambled, but I'm better now that I'm out from under the watchful eye of Nurse Ratched," Ridley told him and fastened his seat belt.

"Well don't get too cocky there, Mr. Scrambled Eggs, you're under my watchful eye now and I can be a tyrant."

"Hey," Ridley protested. "I thought you were my hero, not my warden."

"One and the same," Alex said slyly.

"Great," he muttered. Ridley tried looking out the window, but the flashing scenery made his head throb so he closed his eyes and leaned back against the seat.

"You okay?" Alex asked, sounding concerned.

"Yeah, I'm fine, just exhausted," Ridley assured him without opening his eyes. "I don't think I got more than an hour of sleep last night."

"You can get a nap while I make breakfast."

"Good luck finding anything to cook at my place," Ridley told him and yawned.

Ridley didn't cook. Rather, he didn't cook well, so he usually always ate out or popped a frozen dinner into the microwave. He didn't even have a pot.

"I figured as much, so I'm taking you to my place."

"Really?" Ridley's eyes flew open and he turned toward Alex. The quick movement caused a dizzying sensation. "Whoa!" he hissed and grabbed his head. He had to close his eyes again, the spinning causing his gut to roil.

"Uh-huh, I see how *fine* you are," Alex chastised. "You're going to have to let the macho-boy shit go and let me take care of you."

"You can take care of me all you want," Ridley said, trying to sound seductive but it came out slightly slurred, groggy sounding.

"Oh good Lord," Alex chuckled.

Ridley didn't respond. If he was a good boy, maybe he'd get what he wanted. He smiled broadly at the thought.

"Here we go," Alex said after he parked and shut off the engine.

Ridley opened his eyes, blinking a few times until his eyes adjusted and the world righted itself. He took in the small Tudor home nestled in a small grove of trees. The house sat back from the road, the yard and structure hidden from the road by large trees and a privacy fence. It was, in a word, quaint, which just didn't seem to fit Alex's personality. "This is your place?"

"Yeah."

"It doesn't fit you," Ridley muttered.

"Why do you say that? It's quiet and remote. It totally fits me," he insisted.

"I would have thought so when I first met you, but now…." Ridley shrugged. "Cute and quaint, doesn't fit you."

"Sure it does," Alex laughed and stepped out of the car.

Alex stayed right at Ridley's side as they went up the front walk to the door. It was a little slow going, Ridley had to keep his head up and clamp down on the nausea, but he made it. He was slow and felt drugged, and no matter how hard he tried to take in his surroundings, he couldn't. He was worse off than he thought because he couldn't focus on anything and the room blurred.

"I think I need to sit down," Ridley said dejectedly. He'd hoped to impress Alex, but he couldn't even stand up on his own, his legs felt like rubber, and if he didn't sit down soon and get his head down between his legs, he was going to upchuck all over Alex's house.

He heard the keys clink against a hard surface and then Alex's arm was around him. "I got ya," he murmured against Ridley's ear.

Ridley flailed a little when Alex pushed him down onto a soft cushion. Saliva pooled in his mouth and he swallowed several times as he fought to keep his gut from spewing. He put his head between his knees and took slow, even breaths, praying he didn't puke. It was close, but with Alex rubbing his back soothingly and a bit of stubbornness on his own part, the nausea eased.

"That was close," he admitted.

"Here, lie back," Alex said gently as he helped Ridley get stretched out on the couch. Ridley winced as pain lanced through his head when it came in contact with the arm of the couch and quickly turned to the side. "Be right back, I'm going to get you some ice for your head."

"Thanks," Ridley mumbled, closed his eyes, and burrowed under the blanket Alex laid over him. Ridley was trembling with the exertion it had taken to get from the car to the house. He really was hurt worse than he wanted to acknowledge, but for the first time he had to finally admit defeat.

CHAPTER 7

"RIDLEY," ALEX said gently.

Ridley tried to respond, to swim to the surface of the stupor he seemed to be in. But he was so warm, so comfortable, and not even Alex's voice could entice Ridley to leave it.

"Come on, you got to wake up."

"I don't want to," Ridley huffed and pulled the covers over his head.

"You have to, doctor's orders," Alex encouraged. "Besides, your breakfast is getting cold."

At first he thought of ignoring Alex. He was perfectly happy and content and knew that as soon as he sat up the nausea and dizziness would return. He was beyond tired of dealing with that shit and would be fine to sleep for the next week until the swelling in his fucked-up head went down. Apparently, Alex had other ideas.

"Let's go," he said with a little more force to his tone and pulled the covers off.

"Stop being mean to me," Ridley grumbled and swatted weakly at him. "I have a broken head. For the love of God, take pity on me."

"Pity is for pansies. Now open them eyes and let me see those peepers." Alex patted Ridley's face softly. "C'mon, let me see them."

He grunted in irritation but did as Alex instructed and then whimpered pathetically when the light stung his eyes. He closed them again. "Just leave me alone in my misery, okay?"

"No can do. But if you don't get up and eat this yummy omelet, hash browns, and toast I slaved away to make you, I'm going to make some plain ol' boring oatmeal and force-feed it to you."

Ridley's stomach growled, reminding him he hadn't eaten since the night before. The idea of oatmeal being forced down his throat made him open his eyes. He hated oatmeal, thought the texture was gross. "Damn, you're worse than Nurse Old Fart," he groaned.

"Yeah well, I bet she can't cook like me. Now suck it up, buttercup, and sit up."

Ridley rubbed a hand over the stubble on his chin and then across his burning eyes.

"C'mon!"

"Shut up," Ridley huffed. "Give me a minute."

Alex didn't comment on the crass words, nor did he take pity and give him the desired minute. Instead, he grabbed Ridley's arm and tugged.

"Fuck," Ridley groaned as he was pulled to a sitting position.

"That comes after you get better, but first, food," Alex said and shoved a heaping plate at Ridley. "Start with this. I'll go get your juice and coffee."

Ridley was about to protest on general principle about the rough treatment, but the delicious scents wafting up had him clamping down on the complaint and grabbing the fork.

"Good boy," Alex chuckled and headed to the kitchen.

"I'll show you good boy," Ridley said around a large bite of omelet. Right after he got his legs back. However, he wasn't worried about showing off at the moment, he was starved. He shoveled in another large bite and hummed happily as he chewed.

"You might not want to eat so fast," Alex commented, coming back into the room and handing Ridley a glass of orange juice.

"Thanks," he grunted and downed half the juice.

"Okay, you stubborn shit, ignore my warning, but when you end up going Exorcist on me, you get to clean up the projectile vomit," Alex said.

"Oh!" Ridley answered and set the glass on the side table. "Eww, yeah, I'm really not up to cleaning up puke."

Alex set a steaming cup of coffee next to the juice, then took a seat next to Ridley. "Mmmhmm, I thought you'd see it my way."

"This is really good," he praised and took another bite, smaller this time, and chewed slowly, savoring it.

"Thanks. How are you feeling?"

"The room's not spinning and I don't feel as if I'm about to puke, so I'd say that is a hell of an improvement from earlier. Head still hurts, but not too bad."

"There was a script for some pain pills attached to your discharge instructions. If you feel up to it after you eat, we can run to the pharmacy. I don't want to leave you alone."

"Nah. I mean I'm up to it, but I don't want them. This is the first time since last night I don't feel as if I'm on a tilt-a-whirl. A couple Tylenol will work if you got 'em."

"Sure, be right back."

Ridley took a few more bites, then set his plate aside and picked up his coffee. He was completely and unapologetically addicted to coffee, and the first sip of the warm brew made him moan. He was sure the headache was from more than just a crack on the head. He was going through caffeine withdrawal. He took another big gulp.

Alex came back into the room with his own mug of coffee and sat back down next to Ridley. "Ask and ye shall receive," he said and held out the pills.

"Blow job," Ridley responded and swallowed the medicine.

"What?" Alex looked at him with a confused expression.

"You said ask and ye shall receive," Ridley reminded him and waggled his brows seductively.

Alex laughed and shook his head.

"Totally for medicinal purposes, I assure you. Haven't you heard the best thing for a headache is an orgasm?"

"I've heard that," Alex chuckled into his mug. "You be a good boy and follow your discharge instructions, and we'll test the theory for accuracy later."

"Why wait?" Ridley asked with a tilt of his head. "No time like the present, I always say."

"Because the doctor said no exertion and to stay calm. Trust me, my blow jobs do anything but create a calming effect," Alex said confidently.

"I hate him," Ridley grumbled.

"Poor baby," Alex placated. "How about I make it up to you by giving you a bath?"

"Mmm," Ridley said, perking up. "Then can I have the blow job?" Screw doctor's orders, his dick was hardening and he was getting all tingly.

"We'll see," Alex said smugly as he collected the dirty dishes. "You sit back and let your food digest and I'll get the water running."

Ridley only had a small stand-up shower at his place and hadn't gotten to soak in a hot bath in forever. With or without the blow job, he was looking forward to it, although a little lip-to-dick would definitely make it all the more pleasurable.

Ridley stretched out and for the first time was able to take in Alex's home. He suddenly realized why he hadn't picked up anything while having breakfast. There was nothing there, nothing to see. Sure, there was a couch and a couple of end tables, but that was it. No TV, no design elements or personal effects. The walls were stark white, no personality anywhere to be found. He'd learned quickly Alex didn't like to share personal information, but this place just didn't fit what he knew of the man. Ridley thought that at the very least there would have been a bookshelf full of books, a book bag, something, but it was as sterile as the hospital room he'd just left.

"Tub's drawn," Alex called from the other room. "You need some help?"

"Nah, I'm good," Ridley assured him.

He shifted on the couch, putting his feet on the floor. The movement caused his head to throb, but the room wasn't going all wonky, which made him ridiculously happy. Sure he'd be fine but still cautious, Ridley slowly stood and his confidence plummeted right along with his churning gut as the pain in his head intensified and the room began to spin.

"Whoa," he groaned and grabbed his head in both hands as he fell back onto the couch.

A rumbling sound had him lolling his head to the side, and after a few seconds his vision focused on Alex who was leaning against the doorway chuckling. "I thought as much."

"Then why in the hell did you ask?" Ridley complained.

"Because you think you're a badass motherfucker and who am I to argue with you?"

"I am a badass motherfucker," he grumped. "But I have a very serious head injury so that title is temporarily on hold." Ridley tried to sound cool and gruff, but it came out as more of a whimper and a moan.

Alex obviously caught his feeble attempt as well because he was still laughing when he headed over to help Ridley to his feet.

"I've changed my mind. I think I'll just stay here, wallow in my own filth, and sleep," Ridley mumbled, laid his head back, and closed my eyes.

Alex grabbed Ridley's hand and tugged. "Nope, you have to stay awake for at least another hour so you might as well get clean."

He shoved at Alex's grip, refusing to budge or open his eyes. "Stop being mean to me. I'm an injured man. You can't treat the infirm this way. It's heartless."

"Doctor's orders," Alex said, still tugging on him.

"I won't tell him if you won't." He found enough reserved strength to pull his hand free from Alex's.

"Oh no you don't," Alex growled and grabbed onto Ridley's forearm before he could snuggle down into the couch. "Up and at 'em."

Ridley grudgingly let Alex pull him to his feet and clung to the man when his knees began to buckle. "How about you just drop me off at home and let me die alone," he groaned pathetically.

"You're not going to die and I'm not taking you home until you can at least walk on your own."

"I don't need to walk. I just need to get horizontal and stay that way," Ridley countered but it was a weak attempt. He was too busy focusing on not landing on his ass and trying to ignore the little flashes of light zinging around his vision.

Once in the bathroom, Alex helped Ridley with his clothes and then held onto him while Ridley eased down into the warm bathwater. He sighed as he was submerged in the warm, sudsy water. Ridley would have thought he'd be hard and ready after being undressed by his wet dream, especially when Alex grabbed a washcloth and started washing Ridley's chest. However, his injuries were a more immediate concern, and he leaned back against the tub, closed his eyes, and let the heat and calm ease his throbbing head.

Ridley lay there with the scents of sandalwood and heather filling his nostrils and the silkiness of the soap soft against this flesh. It felt amazing to be pampered, but still…. "Why are you doing this for me?" he asked because he really wanted to know.

"Because you're hurt and need help," Alex said, sounding matter-of-fact.

Ridley opened his eyes and stared at him. "That's nice of you, but I didn't think you wanted to see me again?"

"Why would you think that?" Alex questioned without meeting his gaze.

"Well, let's see, there is the little matter of you being gone when I woke up, no note, nothing. Then the fact that you weren't at work the week after we spent the night together." He ticked each one off on his fingers. "And not to mention you haven't returned my texts or calls. Hmm, I don't know why I would think you didn't want to see me again."

Alex dropped the washcloth in the tub, grabbed a hand towel, and sat on the commode while he dried his hands. He still hadn't looked at Ridley so it was hard to read his expression.

After a long-drawn-out moment, Alex finally sighed heavily. "I didn't plan on seeing you again."

Even though Ridley already suspected it, hearing it, having it confirmed hurt—like stick a knife in his gut and twist kind of pain. Fortunately, in his pitiful state, he didn't think Alex noticed his disappointment. Rejection sucked, but it had never bothered him as much as it did coming from Alex.

"So again I ask, why are you taking care of me now?"

"Because I feel a bit responsible for what happened."

"I'm the one who jumped in without calculating all the risks. You're not responsible nor is there anything for you to feel guilty about," Ridley assured him. "I'm sure I can get Rae to stay with me. You don't have to take care of me and I'll leave you alone."

"Look, Ridley, it's nothing personal. I like you and we had fun, but I'm not sure I'm the…." He shrugged. "I'm not really boyfriend material."

"Boyfriend?" Ridley nearly choked on his surprise and coughed to cover it up. Hell yeah, Alex intrigued him more than any guy he'd ever hooked up with and he could easily admit he found himself thinking about Alex a lot. But boyfriend? "I'm just looking for someone to hang out with, have a beer, shoot a game of pool, and enjoy some hot, kinky sex. I'm a college student, for Christ sake, not looking to get fucking married." He arched a brow at Alex. "If you haven't noticed, the pond of hot gay men in this town isn't actually a pond, more like a puddle."

Alex tilted his head and met Ridley's gaze. His lip curled into a sly grin. "Hot, kinky sex, huh?"

The seductive lilt of Alex's voice and the glint of mischief in his eyes caused Ridley to get all tingly again. "The kinkier the better."

"Then you better work on healing that broken head of yours," Alex drawled with a wink, dropped the towel on the floor, and walked out the door.

"Hey, where are you going?" Ridley called after him. "My other head is in perfect working condition." He looked down to where his hardening dick was straining upward, the head in question peeking up out of the water. "Come back here!"

Alex's response was a deep rumbling chuckle. *Bastard.* He wasn't all that upset when Alex didn't come back; after all, Alex was merely forcing Ridley to follow doctor's orders. He was relieved they'd gotten the little issue of boyfriend and expectations out of the way. Maybe now they could actually start hanging out and having some fun. Plus, the tub was relaxing as hell and his throbbing head had quieted. And seeing as he had a whole bottle of body wash and a more-than-capable hand.... "What the hell," he murmured and wrapped a fist around his cock and stroked it. From the look Alex had given him, he was sure there would be plenty of time to explore the kinky later. For now he'd start thinking of all the things he wanted to explore with the sexy fucker.

Ridley sank farther down in the tub and stroked himself again.

CHAPTER 8

OTHER THAN keeping up on his studies, Ridley did nothing strenuous as per doctor's orders—surprisingly—for the next week. He rarely did what he was told; rather, he tended to do what he wanted, when he wanted. But he quickly discovered that a cracked head was some seriously scary shit. He'd always thought concussions were an excuse athletes used to take the night off. Now he knew better. The headaches and dizziness subsided within a couple of days, but holy hell he just didn't feel right all week. He was withdrawn, confused, had a hard time remembering, concentrating, and was tired, like really fricking tired, even after a full night of sound sleep. He had a new respect for those athletes because it for real sucked.

The one good thing during the week of infirmity was the texts he got from Alex first thing each morning and last thing each evening. They were generally not much more than *Good morning* or *Good night*, but they never failed to make Ridley smile. Actually, it wasn't the only good thing. Rae—while irritatingly motherly—was pretty awesome and the main reason he was up and about and heading to the library to see Alex.

He'd promised Rae he'd call his parents, tell them about the injury before they started getting the statements from the insurance company, but first he needed to get the hell out of his stuffy apartment, clear his mind. The conversation with Mom so wasn't going to go well. But he'd worry about that later. The cool spring breeze and early-morning sun felt good on his face. He pulled on his shades and hummed as he made his way across campus. He could have easily done his studies from home, but he was going batshit stir-crazy, the walls of his place closing in on him.

Besides, he really wanted to see a sexy library assistant even more than he wanted to ace his exam. And damn sure more than he wanted to hear the guilt trip his mom was going to put on him. He had messed-up priorities, sure, but he was smitten or horny or both. Whatever, he was all zipped up to see Alex.

He rounded the corner and nearly slammed into Kyle Bouche. His normally handsome face was swollen, below both eyes was an ugly mix of red, purple and yellow, and he had tape across his nose.

"Whoa there," Ridley grunted and grabbed onto Kyle's jacket before they both ended up on their asses.

Kyle's eyes went wide, a horrified expression on his face. He spun, ripping his jacket from Ridley's grasp, and took off hobbling and limping in the direction he'd just come from.

"What the fuck, man?"

Ridley knew he was tough, had a bit of a badass vibe going on with the piercings, tats, and epic clothing choices, but he didn't have a rep for being scary. He was more the quiet kind of badass with a "don't fuck with me, I won't fuck with you" attitude. And he wasn't the one who had done that to Kyle's face. Seeing Kyle looking so scared, probably pissing himself as he half ran, half limped, was unsettling. *What all had happened that night?* The whole thing was just... weird.

As soon as he walked through the door of the library, Ridley caught sight of Alex waving from where he was standing next to the front desk. He was dressed in a pair of jeans and a long-sleeved white Henley, nothing special, but.... The images of Alex, both dressed and undressed, had been seared into Ridley's brain, but for some reason he looked even sexier than Ridley remembered after not seeing him for a week. For a moment he forgot all about the run-in with Kyle, school, exams, what day of the week it was. It sounded lame, but it was nonetheless true.

"Hey, Alex," he said in greeting as he moved to stand next to him.

Alex leisurely ran his gaze up and down Ridley's body. Ridley discreetly pushed out his chest and stood a little taller. "Looking good," Alex responded with a wink. "How ya feeling?"

"Well, I can bend over and tie my shoes without doing a face plant and I can remember what I had for breakfast. Still dizzy, but the room no longer spins."

He couldn't help but smile at the sound of Alex's laugh. He might have noticed it once or ten times, but Alex had a really, really great laugh.

"That's good to know." Alex raised his soda bottle and took a long drink.

Ridley's gaze was instantly drawn to Alex's throat, the way his Adam's apple bobbed. He'd been excited about seeing Alex, horny as fuck actually, but was still shocked at how incredibly fast his arousal was spiking. Ridley forced his gaze away from that sexy working, swallowing throat and the fantasies it inspired. He shoved his hands in his coat pockets, pushing it down to hide the effect the man was having on him. The library was really no place to be popping a boner.

"So, how has your week been?" Ridley asked, needing a subject change, something other than his dick to focus on.

"It's been crazy. Working, studying, exams."

Alex screwed the cap back on his bottle, and Ridley got a good look at the thick scabs on the knuckles of Alex's right hand. Ridley had hoped as the swelling in his head went down, his recollection of the fight would return, but it hadn't. He had so many questions. Like why Kyle was suddenly scared shitless of him. Why the cops weren't showing up on his doorstep or hauling him in for a full statement? What had happened to Kyle and his goons and how in the hell Alex had come out of the whole mess with nothing more than some scraped knuckles? Problem was, Alex wasn't much of a talker, and any time Ridley tried to talk about anything other than fucking, the man closed up like a steel trap. Ridley knew scarcely more about Alex than when he'd first met him, which only made his curiosity grow.

What hell are you hiding behind that geekish appearance and calm demeanor? "Any more problems?" he inquired and nodded toward the damage on Alex's knuckles.

Alex's brows rose and he looked down at his hands as if he didn't know what Ridley was talking about. He shook his head. "Hey, I gotta go get clocked in," he murmured without meeting Ridley's gaze, something he was learning Alex did when he didn't want to talk. "You going to be around for a while?"

"Yeah. I have a make-up test I need to study for."

"Umm.... Okay.... Good," Alex muttered, sounding distracted as he scanned the area, looking everywhere but at Ridley. "I'll hit you up later."

Ridley watched as Alex walked away, his normal confident swagger jerky.

Ridley took in the library but didn't see anything or anyone unusual. With a shrug he headed to one of the empty tables, chalking up the uneasy feeling that was skittering along his spine as a lingering effect of the concussion. He knew it was more than that, but he was unwilling to let it damper his excitement in seeing Alex.

He tried concentrating on his studies but found himself constantly seeking out Alex, thinking about him and what had happened. He obviously had no problems focusing, only his attention was on the wrong subject. He couldn't get the look on Kyle's face out of his head. Alex had put a hell of a beatdown on the guy, and Ridley suspected it was Alex who had made Kyle so afraid of him, but how?

"You going to hang out here all day?"

Ridley jerked his head up and found Alex smiling. He'd been so deep in thought for the last—he checked the wall clock—two hours. *Wow.* More amazing was he hadn't even been aware of Alex's presence. "I.... Uh, yeah.... Sorry was... was daydreaming."

"You okay?" Alex's smile fell, a concerned expression taking its place.

"Oh yeah, fine," Ridley assured him. "Theory and application of structural analysis has a way of scattering my brain," he lied and pointed to his laptop screen.

Alex cocked his head and studied him as if he were a bug under a microscope. Was he looking for hints of deception? He had the strange feeling Alex was pulling away the layers, discovering the secrets buried under each one. A droplet of sweat rolled down Ridley's temple and his heart rate quickened, but he refused to look away. He also tried not to squirm while keeping his expression light and carefree, but it was difficult. As Alex continued to stare, analyze him, Ridley took the opportunity to do the same. To *really* look at the man, not just the handsome features. Alex had a small cut above his left eye, partially hidden in his brow, but it had taken quite a few stitches to close as indicated by the spotted scar. His nose had a bump and turned slightly to the right. It appeared as if it had been broken more than once. But there was something in his eyes, something deep. Sorrow? Anger? Regret? All of the above? Ridley wasn't sure, but one thing he was sure of was that there was wisdom in those eyes, knowledge normally only seen in a man or woman who had lived twice as long as Alex.

Alex suddenly spun as if someone from behind had called out to him, though Ridley hadn't heard anyone. "Library closes in an hour," Alex grumbled and strode away. Alex walked across the library, his steps quick, with purpose. He never even looked back, simply disappeared into the office and slammed the door.

"What the fuck just happened?" Ridley muttered under his breath and ran a hand through his sweat-dampened hair.

Everyone around him still had their noses buried in books or was writing frantically. A couple of girls had their heads close, hands over their mouths, giggling. No one seemed to have noticed the intense moment he'd just had with Alex, one that left Ridley trembling. It was as if he'd been dropped into some strange, unknown place and had no idea what to do next.

This was going to drive him crazy: the uneasy feelings, the secrets, Alex's refusal to talk about what had happened. How the hell was he supposed to get to know the man if he wouldn't talk to him? No, he didn't have to know him to fuck him, but dammit, he'd like for him and Alex to not only be fuck buddies but also friends. Ridley drummed his fingers against the tabletop. Yeah, he was also a bit intrigued... okay, a lot intrigued. Where did someone who looked like Alex learn to fight, and how in the hell could a geeky library assistant instill so much fear in Kyle?

Decision made, Ridley stuffed his laptop into his backpack. Somehow he had to do the same thing Alex had been doing to him. Ridley would just have to peel back the layers on Alex and find the secrets beneath. Sex and alcohol might just help him get a couple of those layers lifted.

CHAPTER 9

RIDLEY LEANED against the railing watching Alex tromp down the steps of the library. The moment Alex noticed Ridley, his brows furrowed and he scanned the area around them.

"Hey, Ridley," Alex said in greeting, the wary expression giving way to a slight grin. "Fancy meeting you here."

"Was just out for a stroll, hoping to find a little companionship for the night."

"Is that so?" Alex snorted. "Most guys don't scope out the library for dates."

"Most libraries don't have hot assistants working in them. Can I interest you in a drink?"

"I...." Alex looked up and down the street as if he were looking for someone.

"Oh, if you already have plans—"

"No, that's not it," Alex interrupted. "I'm just not sure hanging out in a bar is the best idea right now. You know"—he shrugged—"with what happened the other night."

"What did happen the other night?" Ridley pressed.

"You got yourself knocked upside the head. I got some booze and snacks at my place," Alex said, quickly changing the subject. "No pool table but I'm sure we can find another game to wager on."

Ridley was suspicious of the way Alex continued to take in his surroundings, his eyes constantly moving as if he were watching for someone, but who? It couldn't be a date if he was asking Ridley back to his place. Was it Kyle? That seemed unlikely considering the way Kyle had behaved earlier. The man had been scared shitless, and the chances he'd be looking for or going after Alex seemed highly unlikely. His curiosity piqued, Ridley started to press Alex about the events of the other night, but changed his mind. He'd work on that later, after a few shots to loosen Alex's tongue.

"What kind of game did you have in mind?" Ridley settled on.

"Strip poker?"

"Hmm, I'm pretty good at poker."

"I do like a challenge. Let's go." Alex nodded to the right and they headed down the sidewalk.

For being only nine at night, the streets were oddly deserted. It was a weeknight, so Ridley expected the crowds to be light, but it seemed strange to be this dead. "Anything going on tonight?"

"Yeah. I'm going to get drunk and win me a pile of clothes."

"I do like your confidence." Ridley sniffed and bumped his shoulder against Alex's. "But I meant in town. Where the hell is everyone?"

"No clue. I don't really pay attention to much of the extracurricular shit that goes on around here," Alex admitted.

"Hmm, me neither, but I've never seen it this quiet."

"Maybe it's finals that's got everyone home cramming for exams," Alex suggested.

It was plausible, although finals weren't for another couple of weeks, but Ridley shrugged it off.

They crossed the road at the corner, and Alex pulled out his key fob and hit the button. The lights on his car flashed in the parking lot. "You got your car here?" Alex asked.

"No, I walked."

"You want to ride with or would you rather meet me at my place?"

Ridley thought about it for a second. On one hand, if he had his car he could sneak out in the morning if so inclined. On the other, he knew he wouldn't want to be sneaking out anywhere and the thought of waking up with Alex was quite appealing.

"I'll ride with you, if that's okay?"

"Sure, I wouldn't have asked otherwise." Alex opened the passenger door and ushered Ridley in. "Your chariot awaits you, good sir."

"Sexy, tough, and polite," Ridley mused as he slid into the passenger seat and buckled in.

"I'm the complete package," Alex informed him before he shut the door.

No, the complete package would be if you were boyfriend material. The idea shocked Ridley. Where the hell had that come from?

Alex ran around the front of the car and slid in behind the wheel and started the car up. He cocked his head at Ridley. "You look like you've just seen a ghost," he said, sounding confused.

"You could say that." Ridley shook his head. Man, he was all over the place lately. A total flake. He shook his head again. "I'm good. So, about that game?"

"You sure you're not still feeling the effect of your concussion?" Alex asked once he got them heading down the road.

"Nah, I'm good. Doc gave me a clean bill of health," he assured him. "Though I still don't remember too much about the fight," he admitted.

"Not much to remember. You jumped, got hit, knocked out cold, and I called the ambulance."

Ridley shifted in his seat so he was facing Alex a little more directly. "But what happened after I got hit?"

"You got knocked out," Alex deadpanned.

"Yes, so you've told me and then you called the ambulance. But what happened between the time I got hit and the call?"

Alex tapped his thumbs on the steering wheel. From the guarded expression on his face, he was choosing his words carefully.

"Why is it such a secret?" Ridley prompted.

"Not really a secret, nor much to tell."

"I don't believe that. C'mon, Alex, you don't take on five guys on your own and come away with just a few scraped-up knuckles. Where did you learn to fight like that?"

"I didn't take on five. You took out one," he pointed out.

Ridley gave Alex an exasperated look. "Seriously, dude, where did you learn to fight like that?"

"I was always a bit of a scrapper. Used to drive my mom and dad nuts. This one time I got kicked out of junior high school for five days and then the day I was allowed back, got kicked out for fighting again. My dad tore my ass up for that one."

"Really?"

"Yup," Alex laughed. "Couldn't sit down for a week without feeling the sting."

"You just don't seem the type."

"I was a bit high-strung."

"Why don't I believe this story?" Ridley said suspiciously. "And even if it's true, scrapping in junior high is a long way from taking on five big jocks by yourself in an alleyway."

"I told you—"

"Okay, fine," Ridley relented. "Four."

"Don't know how I can convince you. Want my mom's phone number?"

"Yes."

Alex stared at him wide-eyed for a second before turning his attention back to the road. "Wow, you really don't trust me, do you?"

"I don't know if it has anything to do with trust. I'm just trying to figure you out."

"Don't try," Alex said curtly.

"Why is that?"

"You won't like what you discover." The hard set to Alex's jaw and the harsh tone of his voice told Ridley he'd pushed the man far enough.

The tension in the car was instantly thick, nearly palpable. Ridley was far from done with this conversation, but he'd let it go. For now.

The rest of the ride to Alex's place was made in silence. Ridley half expected Alex to turn around and take Ridley home, so he was surprised when they pulled into Alex's driveway and he cut the engine. Neither of them said a word or made a move for a long moment, the tension increasing with each tick of the clock.

"I'm sorry—"

"C'mon in," Alex said at the same time. He ignored Ridley's attempt to apologize for putting a damper on the evening and stepped out of the car. Ridley followed him up the walk. Alex's movements were once again jerky, something Ridley was beginning to recognize as something Alex did when irritated or wary.

Alex unlocked the front door and pushed it open, allowing Ridley to enter first. Alex shut the door behind them, and the room suddenly pitched into complete darkness without the glow of the porch light.

"Shh," Alex whispered.

Ridley stood stock-still and held his breath as his pulse began to race, and he strained to listen for anything out of the ordinary. He heard nothing. What the hell was going on?

Ridley jerked when his hair was pulled, and before he could protest, his mouth was covered and Alex's tongue was pushing deep. A thrill of fear and danger raced down Ridley's spine, causing him to shiver.

GODDAMN THIS was a bad, bad, bad idea. His dick was going to get Alex in trouble again, but even as he thought it, he was deepening the kiss. He knew better and yet here he was. He curled his fist in Ridley's hair, tilting his head for better access as he devoured the man's delicious mouth. He'd used the kiss to cover up the fact that he'd hesitated to listen for any movement within his house, for not turning on a light. Alex should be checking the house out, not standing here in the dark fucking Ridley's mouth with his tongue, but shit that man was irresistible. A bonus was the way Ridley was responding and not asking any more questions Alex was unable to answer. It was going to make it that much harder to leave Ridley, but at least they would have this one more time.

Alex continued to explore, licking and nipping at Ridley's mouth for another moment until he pulled a deep moan from the man. Only then did he end the kiss and flip on the light switch.

Their mouths still only an inch apart, Ridley blinked against the sudden light and licked his lips. "Well now," he murmured.

Holding Ridley's gaze, Alex released Ridley's hair and ran his hand down Ridley's rapidly rising and falling chest to his groin. Alex cupped Ridley's erection and gave it a squeeze. "What can I get you to drink?"

Ridley pushed into Alex's touch. "Whatever you're having," he responded, a little breathless.

"Bourbon," Alex said with a wink and stepped away. He heard Ridley groan behind him and smiled.

On the way to the kitchen, he ran a critical eye over the area. Everything looked as he'd left it, no signs anyone had been there, no light tripped on the movement sensor. He retrieved two glasses from the cabinet and a bottle of bourbon and set them on the island. After adding ice to the glasses, he poured them each a generous amount and handed one to Ridley as he joined Alex in the kitchen.

Alex took a healthy gulp, keeping his eyes on Ridley as he did so. The man looked a little stunned, a little off balance, and a whole lot horny. Good. He'd use it to his advantage to keep Mr. Too-Many-Questions from asking any more tonight.

"That's just the warm-up. I think I have a deck of cards here somewhere." Alex set his glass down and started rummaging through a drawer.

"Right to the games, huh?"

Alex shrugged. "If you'd rather get right to the fucking, that works for me too."

Ridley choked on his bourbon. "Nothing like getting right to the point."

Alex found what he was looking for and slid the cards from their box. "I'm not big on games."

Ridley looked at the cards in Alex's hand, then back up and arched a brow.

"Okay, let me rephrase that," he snorted. "I'm not big on games unless they lead to fucking."

"Well then by all means, deal 'em," Ridley encouraged and took a seat in one of the barstools across from Alex.

Alex dealt out five cards each and set the deck aside. "Five-card stud," Alex announced and picked up his cards and studied them. A pair of jacks. "I wager my shirt."

Ridley flipped over his cards without looking at them first. "Call."

Ridley had an ace and nothing else. Alex threw his cards down. "Hand it over," he demanded and made a gimme motion with his hand.

Alex refilled their glasses as Ridley pulled his T-shirt over his head and handed it over as instructed. Alex's gaze roamed appreciatively over Ridley's muscular chest. His muscles were taut, the skin smooth, his dark nipples erect, causing Alex's mouth to water. "Very nice," he said seductively.

Ridley pushed out his chest, then ran a hand across his chest and pinched one of the dark nubs. "Thanks."

"Oh, you are asking for it," Alex said warningly.

"Yes I am," Ridley responded and waggled his brows.

Alex had damn sure picked the right topic to take Ridley's mind off all the questions. Alex knew Ridley's inquisitive mind wouldn't let it drop, but for now it was another head that was making the decisions and Alex would use that to his full advantage.

Alex dealt them each five more cards from the stack. "I want your pants this time," he told him.

"Gonna be hard to get them off over my shoes," Ridley chuckled and picked up his cards. A large grin spread across his face. Obviously Ridley had a good hand. The man had no face for poker.

"Fine," Alex relented. "But shoes and socks count as one."

"Deal," Ridley agreed and laid his cards face up on the table. "Take 'em off." Ridley picked up his drink and leaned back in his chair, a satisfied grin on his face.

While Ridley sipped at his drink, Alex studied Ridley's cards. He had two pairs, threes and nines. Alex flipped his over, not so much as a pair. He kicked off his shoes and then bent and pulled off his socks. He laid them on the counter.

"Thank you very much," Ridley drawled and pulled them closer to him. "Deal."

"Now who is ready to get right down to it?"

"You started it," Ridley snorted. "Deal," he repeated.

Regardless of who won the card game, Alex was going to enjoy wiping that smug grin off Ridley's face when he fucked him through the mattress. Alex adjusted the bulge in his jeans and then grabbed the stack of cards. He started to toss one to Ridley facedown.

"Faceup this time. I like a little anticipation."

"Enjoy your demands while you can." Alex smirked and flipped over the card. Ace.

"Is that a threat?" Ridley challenged.

"Think of it as a promise," he informed Ridley and turned over his own card. King.

Slowly, Alex turned one card over at a time. Ridley was right, the anticipation made it all the more exciting. By the time Alex had dealt them each five cards and saw he had the winning hand with two kings, his pulse was beating a little faster.

Ridley removed his socks and shoes without question and shoved them across the counter without saying a word.

Ridley lost the next hand as well. He stood and popped the button on his jeans.

"Slowly," Alex demanded. He downed the rest of his bourbon. "Give me a show."

"A show?"

"Yeah, anticipation makes everything better, remember?"

"That it does," Ridley agreed and ran his hand over the front of his jeans.

Alex's gaze was riveted to the movement and the flex and roll of the muscles in Ridley's colorfully inked arm as he pressed his palm against his cock, stroking himself a few times before he eased down the zipper. His hands on the waistband of his jeans, Ridley then turned his back to Alex and swayed. Instead of pushing down the denim fabric, the little tease raised his arms over his head, and the movement caused the muscles in his back to bulge as he continued to sway to some silent tune only Ridley could hear.

Without taking his gaze from Ridley, Alex poured another shot and gulped it down. He wasn't sure which was having the greater effect on him, the bourbon or the dance, but heat surged through him pleasantly and he liked it.

Finally, Ridley pushed down his jeans a little, first the lighter skin of his ass visible and then the top of his crack. "Commando, huh? I fucking love that," Alex murmured.

Ridley looked back over his shoulder, a mischievous smirk on his face, and wiggled his ass. "That would make you the winner, huh?"

"Damn right," Alex growled, his arousal making his voice harsh.

"Can't make it that easy for you," Ridley laughed and shoved down his jeans to expose his black boxer briefs.

"Another thing you're going to pay for," Alex groaned and grudgingly snatched up the cards.

Ridley stepped out of his jeans and kicked them aside before turning back around. Alex groaned again and his cock throbbed when he got sight of the impressive bulge straining against the cotton material of Ridley's briefs.

Ridley put his hands on his hips with his fingers pointing downward, framing his dick, and swayed back and forth seductively. "See something you like?"

"Yeah," Alex snarled and threw a card—two of clubs—on the counter. "I'm going to like it a whole lot more when I have my fist wrapped around it denying you an orgasm."

Ridley froze.

CHAPTER 10

THE GLINT in Alex's eyes caused a thrill to race down Ridley's spine and he shuddered. The movement of his gyrating hips stopped and he eased down into his chair.

"Don't let me stop your little teasing dance. Please continue," Alex remarked and turned over his card without looking at it.

Ridley downed the last of his bourbon and pushed his glass toward Alex. "No, no, that's quite all right," Ridley said as the booze burned all the way down to his gut. "I was getting a little parched."

"Mmmhmm," Alex hummed, sounding unconvinced. He flipped another card and then refilled Ridley's glass. "Last hand," he pointed out.

"Last hand if you win," Ridley countered.

"You lost that right. Last hand," Alex repeated. "You win, I'll let you come."

Alex flipped another card and added it to the ones in front of Ridley. He looked down to see a four, a six, and a pair of twos. Ridley's heart started to hammer in his chest. "And if you win?"

"You won't."

Ridley studied Alex's cards. Eight, seven, jack, and an ace. "What do you mean 'you won't'?" Ridley asked in confusion.

"You won't be coming," Alex said curtly.

"How the hell are you going to achieve that? He's kind of got a mind of his own, in case you haven't noticed."

Alex flipped over Ridley's last card. The queen added nothing to his hand, but he still had a chance with the pair. Alex looked up from the cards slowly and met Ridley's gaze, the glint in his blue eyes turning into a smoldering fire. "Fuck, I love it when you challenge me."

The deep, husky tone of Alex's voice along with the look in his eyes, the hint of danger, caused Ridley's already rapidly beating heart to race.

Instead of flipping his last card, Alex picked up his glass and held it up. "Here's to Lady Luck."

He waited until Ridley picked his up and then Alex clinked their glasses together and drank his shot in one large gulp. He slammed the glass on the counter and flipped his card.

Ridley didn't look right away. Instead he finished his drink, winced with the burn, and then.... *Fuck!* He knew by the large smile spread across Alex's face that the man had won. Sure enough, there on the counter was the ace of hearts.

"Well, well, well," Alex drawled. "Looks like it's my lucky night. Yours? Not so much." He smirked.

"You weren't actually serious about that bet, were you?" Ridley asked disbelievingly. Alex wouldn't actually deny him an orgasm, would he? Ridley had to admit, however, with the way his dick was pulsing and his flesh tingling, he actually was looking forward to seeing how this would play out.

"Take off the briefs, put your hands flat on the counter, and spread your legs shoulder width apart," Alex said in response to Ridley's question.

"But—"

"Take off the briefs and get into position," Alex interrupted. He didn't look at Ridley. Instead he casually gathered up the cards and returned them to their box.

Ridley hesitated as Alex then picked up the empty glasses and took them to the sink. What would Alex do if Ridley refused? Did he want to know? He'd loved how aggressive Alex had been the last time they were together; did he dare push him further? Yes, he dared, but not on this, not yet.

Ridley stood and shoved his briefs down his legs and kicked them in the direction of his jeans.

"Move the stool out of the way," Alex instructed without turning around as he rinsed out the glasses.

Jesus, the man had eyes in the back of his head. Ridley picked up the stool and set it behind the other one. Sweat blossomed on his brow, and his hands were shaking as he set them on the counter.

Alex made him wait.

Without looking directly at Ridley, Alex finished washing the dishes, dried them, and then returned them to the cupboard. He then picked up the bourbon and returned it as well.

Ridley's legs began to shake, the anticipation surging through him. Once everything was cleaned up, the counters wiped off, Alex walked out of the room. Ridley didn't dare move. He'd learned this last time. This was Alex's game and as long as he played along, he'd be a very, very happy, albeit sore, man come morning.

Alex's steps were silent, but Ridley heard the faint sound of a door opening and closing. Water ran briefly, followed by what sounded like a cabinet clicking shut. There were some additional small, muffled sounds Ridley couldn't place. It felt as if he'd been standing there forever when Alex finally came back into the room. Ridley heard the stereo clicking on behind him. The low sounds of an unfamiliar melody filled the air. It was slow, soothing, but Ridley felt anything but calm. He was literally vibrating with excitement and a little fear, which made the thrill all the sharper, more acute. Ridley was sure it was only moments, ten at the most, before he felt Alex move up behind him. Alex didn't touch him, but Ridley could hear him breathing, feel the heat of Alex's body.

Unable to stand it any longer, Ridley started to push up from the counter when a hard smack landed on his right ass cheek, making him jump.

"Don't move."

"Fuck, that smarts," Ridley hissed.

Another swat landed on his other cheek. "You like the burn."

Ridley didn't even try to deny it. The heat spreading out from his ass, running up his back and down his legs, felt so good he moaned his response.

"Have you ever been tied up and truly dominated?"

"Tied up, no. Dominated? Only once," Ridley admitted.

"Oh, that's right," Alex teased. "You always thought you were the dominant one. The tough one. Makes taking control of you all that much more appealing."

"I wasn't complaining last time," Ridley pointed out. "Might have for a few days afterward but"—he shrugged—"it was worth it."

"I could tell," Alex murmured and moved up closer. Alex obviously had removed his clothes while he'd been in the other room because his hard cock nudged at Ridley's crease. Alex thrust hard against Ridley and his cock pressed snugly in Ridley's crack, rubbing against his asshole. Ridley pressed back against it and moaned.

Alex placed his lips next to Ridley's ear and whispered. "I liked it too. I think I'm going to like what I have planned for tonight even more." He nipped at Ridley's earlobe and then stepped back.

Ridley started to turn in protest, but his hips were grabbed in Alex's vise-like grip and his cheeks were pulled apart. Ridley expected pain, another slap or maybe a dry finger shoved up his ass like last time, but instead what he got was a wet flick of tongue against his opening.

"Oh yeah," Ridley moaned and shoved back against Alex's face.

Alex didn't disappoint. He licked and nipped at Ridley's pucker, his low moans vibrating against Ridley's flesh. Ridley tried to thrust, but with the hold Alex had on him he could only squirm, moan, and beg for more.

"Fucking hell," Ridley cried out when Alex suddenly shoved a finger up Ridley's ass and bit his right cheek.

He should have known the pain was coming, but Alex had lulled him into a false sense of safety. The unexpectedness added a zing to the pain.

"You haven't had anything up this ass since my cock was here, have you?" Alex asked while he corkscrewed his finger inside Ridley.

"No," he confessed.

Alex stabbed his finger in and out of Ridley, twisting with each thrust, nudging Ridley's prostate. "Not a toy?"

"No," Ridley said through gritted teeth.

Alex pulled his finger out till only the tip was breaching Ridley's opening and started moving it in a circular motion. "Not even a finger," Alex murmured.

"Nothing," Ridley assured him.

"Good. I like stretching a nice tight ass."

Ridley cried out again when his other cheek was bitten, but it only seemed to spur Alex on because he started fucking Ridley's ass hard with that finger. As the wetness from Alex mouth began to dry, the friction began to burn, heating Ridley's ass and adding another layer of pain, but it wasn't unpleasant.

"Chest on the counter and grab your ass checks and open yourself for me," Alex demanded, still stabbing that finger in and out faster and faster, harder and harder.

Pulse racing, Ridley dropped his chest to the countertop and gasped at the coldness of the stainless steel against his heated flesh. He grabbed his ass and did as Alex instructed.

"You like being a little slut, don't you?" Alex asked.

"Fuck yeah," Ridley moaned and rocked into the burn.

"Like it raw and dirty."

Alex added another finger, causing Ridley to go up on tiptoes and robbing him of his voice. It hurt like hell, almost too much, and he stopped trying to push against the invading digits, instead instinctively shying away.

Alex pressed a hand against Ridley's lower back, his blunt fingers digging into Ridley's flesh. "Don't you," Alex demanded, continuing to stab in and out of Ridley, spreading his fingers, twisting and turning them.

"Yeah," he got out through his clenched jaw.

Ridley was breathing harshly, his heart hammering as the pain increased to the point where he wasn't sure he could stand it for another second, yet his cock was hard and weeping.

Alex shoved his fingers deep and held them inside Ridley, just barely wiggling them, tickling and teasing Ridley's prostate. The pleasure spiked higher than the pain. "Ah damn," Ridley moaned and tentatively started rocking his hips.

Alex's hand moved with him, pressed snugly against Ridley's cheeks. "I like fucking your ass dry. Like watching you struggle to take it."

"Sick bastard," Ridley grunted in token protest.

Alex reached up between Ridley's legs and grabbed his straining erection, pumping it a few times. "We have that in common," he laughed.

And what the hell was that about? Ridley damn sure couldn't deny it. The evidence was literally in Alex's hand. He'd never been one to be so passive, allow someone to so completely control him. However, just like the last time he'd been with Alex, he was willingly handing him the reins and loving every fucking second of it. Not only loving it, but begging for more.

Alex squeezed Ridley's cock and then released it to bob freely with each movement. The sensation caused Ridley to hump harder, looking for more friction, even though it caused the pain to flare in his ass. He simply couldn't not move.

"Don't want to damage you too much," Alex commented and then something cold and wet hit Ridley's ass, making him gasp. "Not yet anyway." He chuckled wickedly.

Ridley didn't even comment, the slick slip and slide of Alex fingers in and out of Ridley's ass capturing his focus. Alex had obviously squeezed out some lube, which he was working into Ridley, making him thrust even harder as the uncomfortable sensation gave way to pure pleasure.

"You want more?"

"Uh-huh," Ridley muttered and humped harder. His sweat-slick chest slid along the counter as easily as Alex's fingers were sliding in Ridley's ass.

Ridley released his ass, planning on grabbing the edge of the counter to give more leverage to his thrusts, but he quickly aborted the plan when a hard slap landed on his cheek.

"Hands on your ass," Alex demanded.

Ridley instantly did as he was instructed without question.

"I want to watch this."

Ridley didn't need to ask what *this* was. He knew what Alex had in mind when another finger was added to his ass. "Fuck, that's hot," Alex groaned.

"Burns like hell," Ridley complained.

"You like the burn," Alex countered. "In fact, I would wager you're wondering if you could take another one."

"Not at the moment," Ridley hissed as Alex continued thrusting those fat fingers in his ass. He knew he couldn't take another—just two fingers hurt like a son of a bitch, stretching, burning—but still Ridley continued to move against each movement and his cock was still hard as nails. Oh yeah, he was a sick bastard all right.

Thankfully, Alex didn't add another finger, but rather started a fast, even rhythm of fucking Ridley's ass. He also started nibbling and sucking the fingers on Ridley's right hand and then the left, tracing each digit with his tongue.

Once again Ridley allowed himself to be lulled into a false sense of complacency, enjoying the pleasure of Alex's slick fingers, the warmth of his mouth, and tickling sensation of his tongue. A knot formed at the base of his spine, his orgasm beginning to build.

"Ah…. Ah, damn, that feels good," Ridley moaned. His legs trembled as his muscles coiled, tensing in anticipation. "So damn good." And so damn close. He humped harder, chasing his orgasm as his heart hammered in his chest.

The fingers in his ass suddenly disappeared, leaving Ridley feeling empty, but he only had a split second to register the disappointment before his nuts were grabbed in a painful grip and Ridley cried out as fire shot up his spine.

"You didn't win that right," Alex snapped. "You're not to come."

"Motherfucker," he howled, instinctively releasing his ass and reaching for the vise on his sac.

"Ah, ah, ah," Alex tsked, refusing to release him. Curiously, Ridley didn't turn around and punch the son of a bitch. Instead he froze when Alex added, "What's the matter, tough guy?"

It wasn't just what Alex said that had Ridley not reacting but the way he rubbed his lips gently across the cheeks of Ridley's ass. It was in stark contrast to the tone of his voice and the strength of his grip.

"That's better," Alex praised and eased his hold.

The pain flared briefly as sparks of fire fluttered along Ridley's flesh, but then it quickly dulled into warmth. It still shocked Ridley how well Alex could read his body, knowing exactly how far he could push Ridley and exactly when to back off. Even more astonishing was Ridley's reaction to Alex's aggressive and cocky attitude. Why it still shocked him, he wasn't sure. He understood that when he submitted to Alex his orgasm would be tenfold, but Ridley had always been one to want to know the why of things, to understand. Alex turned Ridley's world upside down and left him struggling to keep up. And yet he kept chasing him, wanting him.

"You ready for more?" Alex asked, going to his feet and making his intentions clear when he pressed his hard cock against Ridley's ass.

The need to know why flew out the window. Who cared? "Hell yeah," he responded.

Alex slid his hands beneath Ridley, pulling him back and then wrapping his arms around him. Chest pressed firmly against Ridley's back, cock against his ass, Alex began to sway as his hands roamed along Ridley's chest.

"You drive me out of my goddamn mind," Alex murmured against Ridley's ear. "Make me want to do all kinds of things to you. Naughty things." He nipped Ridley's ear. "Things I know only you can handle."

The praise went straight to Ridley's dick, causing it to throb, and in that second he would have let Alex do anything and everything he wanted. It may have been bullshit, but Alex's comment that Ridley was the *only* one who could handle it made Ridley want to prove he could. "I'm tough enough," Ridley challenged.

"Your body is," Alex agreed. "But is your mind?"

"I don't understand," Ridley countered.

"You will."

Alex released his hold on Ridley, then grabbed his hand and pulled him along. The instant they were in Alex's bedroom, he shoved Ridley toward the bed and then pushed him down on the soft mattress, falling after him and covering Ridley's body with his own.

Alex took Ridley's mouth in a blistering kiss before they even stopped bouncing. Alex rubbed his body against Ridley's like a big cat, a deep rumbling purr emitting from him, and Ridley took the seductive sound into himself and answered it with a hungry moan of his own.

Ridley went still, opened his mouth wide, and let Alex completely control the kiss and the action. A nudge of a knee here, a press of a hand there, and Alex worked Ridley into position until he was spread wide in the center of the bed. Alex held Ridley's arms over his head by his wrists. Only then did Alex end the kiss. Breathing harshly, Alex looked down at Ridley with lust-filled eyes that caused Ridley to shiver.

"I'm going to fuck you till you can't see straight," Alex announced with a sly grin.

Ridley held Alex's gaze for a long-drawn-out moment and then licked his dry lips. "Bring it," Ridley challenged, giving Alex a sly grin of his own.

Alex's eyes narrowed. "On second thought, I'm going to fuck that smug grin right off your face."

"Wasn't that the challenge last time? I thought you would have aimed higher this time," Ridley prodded.

Alex slid his hands down Ridley's arms and planted his hands on Ridley's chest, his expression hardening. "Guess I'm going to have to step up my game, then."

"Guess so," Ridley smirked.

Alex tapped his fingers against Ridley's chest as he rolled his hips, pressing his hardness against Ridley's equally hard shaft. "What to do, where to begin," Alex murmured.

Ridley thrust up, causing them to both hiss. "Need a few suggestions?" he taunted.

"Nah," Alex drawled easily. "I'm just trying to decide what you can and can't handle."

Ridley bucked up even harder. "Try me," he challenged.

Alex pressed the full weight of his lower body down on Ridley, making it virtually impossible for him to move, and pinched both Ridley's nipples simultaneously. Ridley yelped.

"You might want to hold on. It's going to be a hell of a ride," Alex suggested and squeezed hard, sending sparks of pain to race all the way from the hard nubs straight to his cock.

Ridley bit down on his bottom lip to keep from crying out. He stretched his arms farther until they came in contact with the headboard and then wrapped his hands around the metal bars that ran between the wood. It was the only response he gave to Alex's warning. He didn't dare open his mouth to speak. He knew his voice would crack or squeak, and he wanted to do nothing that would give away his façade of tough disbelief.

Alex continued to abuse Ridley's nipples. He pinched, pulled, and rolled them until Ridley was in serious danger of crying out, no doubt the reaction Alex was seeking, but Ridley held fast. He took the pain into himself, rose above it, and found himself literally getting high on it. It was a rush Ridley had never experienced before, at least not to this degree or in this kind of circumstance, and he wanted more.

After a few more seconds of titty torture and still Alex didn't get the reaction he was obviously hoping for, he released Ridley's nipples, shook his head, and chuckled huskily. "Oh, this is going to be fun."

The look in Alex's eyes caused Ridley to swallow hard, but he still managed to speak—now that the pain in his chest was easing to a more bearable level. "Life's too short not to enjoy oneself."

"Truer words were never spoken," Alex commented with a nod.

His heart thumping wildly, Ridley took a deep breath in through his nose and blew it out slowly as Alex reached over and pulled the bedside table drawer open. Ridley didn't know what Alex had done with the lube he'd had in the kitchen, but the man was obviously prepared when he sat back on his calves between Ridley's spread legs, condom and lube in hand.

Ridley watched him intently as Alex opened the foil packet and took his dear sweet time rolling the condom onto his impressive cock. Ridley knew it would do little good to demand or beg Alex to hurry the fuck up. This was part of the game. Alex's game. Ridley released the bars and stretched his fingers before gripping the headboard again. He was trying his damnedest to appear calm, but the rapid rise and fall of his chest was no doubt giving him away.

Alex, the bastard, continued to move at a leisurely pace. He snapped the cap on the lube open and poured a small amount into the palm of his hand. Instead of running it down his straining cock, he dipped a single finger into the lube and ran the tip of that finger slowly around the head of his sheathed cock, an action he continued for the next few minutes until his shaft was liberally lubed up. Only then did he rub his hands together, slicking up his fingers, and then met Ridley's gaze.

"Now we begin," he said wickedly.

CHAPTER 11

RIDLEY PLANTED his feet on the bed, spread his knees, and looked up at Alex, eyes smoldering. There was a blatant challenge on his handsome face.

"You're a brave, brave man," Alex grinned. "Hope it will be worth not being able to walk tomorrow." Laughing, he wedged himself between Ridley's spread thighs and bent low for a bruising kiss, licking and biting at the ring in Ridley's bottom lip, causing him to grunt.

Releasing his hold on the headboard, Ridley pulled his knees up close to his chest, lifted his hips off the bed, and returned the kiss. His hands traveled over Alex's skin, groping, grasping, and digging into soft flesh anywhere they could. "It will be so worth it," he panted.

"I'll ask you the same question tomorrow," Alex said, his voice coming out low and husky. "Hands back on the bars." He grasped his cock and guided it to Ridley's opening.

Ridley did as he was told, his eyes fluttering as Alex breached him. "Don't care. You make me want you so bad, make me fucking nuts with want and need." Ridley's eyes closed and his brow furrowed. "So fucking needy."

Alex shook his head, sliding deeper into Ridley's body. He smiled at the whimper of disappointment when he pulled all the way out.

"God, Alex, would you just fuck me, please," Ridley begged urgently, breathlessly. He rolled his hips higher in an attempt to take Alex deeper. "C'mon, fuck me."

Alex chuckled, then moaned deeply as he pushed in once again. Even with all the ass play, Ridley was tight, squeezing and caressing his cock all the way down the shaft as he plunged deeper. "Oh fuck. Fuck, Ridley," Alex groaned.

"God, Alex, you're so…. Fuck, you're thick," Ridley groaned. "Burns. Hurts so good." He moved gently to the same slow rhythm as Alex's hips, no longer trying to press Alex to move faster now that Alex was buried deep. Ridley leaned up and nipped at Alex's chin and then lazily teased each of Alex's dimples with the tip of his tongue.

With a deep groan Alex moved slowly, the effort it took not to thrust hard and fast causing him to tremble. He kissed Ridley when and where he could as Ridley continued to lavish his cheeks, jaw, and neck with attention. Every nip made his dick throb, working to shred his control.

"You really like that, don't you?" Ridley asked with a grin, though it was more of a statement than a question. "Every time I do this…." He nipped at the skin beneath Alex's chin just hard enough to cause a slight sting. "See? Your cock goes crazy."

Alex's best attempt at a response was a grunt. His cock was twitching wildly and he couldn't seem to get close enough, deep enough. The more he got, the more he wanted. Forcing himself to pull out of Ridley's tight heat, he poised the head of his cock at Ridley's opening. "I like it," he admitted hoarsely. "And you like this." He thrust in again, aiming for Ridley's sweet spot.

Ridley cried out, babbling incoherently. Alex couldn't make out the unintelligible words, but it hardly mattered—he'd obviously hit his target.

He watched as Ridley slid one hand away from the headboard, finding his own shaft and tugging it roughly. "Oh God," he panted. "Do that again."

Alex grinned. "I will if you put your hand back where it belongs," he said, going completely still. Ridley opened his eyes and met Alex's gaze. He huffed out a frustrated breath, gave his cock one last good pull, and then grasped the bar.

As soon as Ridley's hand was back where it belonged, Alex stabbed into Ridley's ass again, ramming himself against Ridley's prostate.

Ridley's breath was warm on his throat as he shouted, and the tickling sensation caused Alex to shiver and moan when Ridley's mouth closed around Alex's Adam's apple. He sucked it hard as he thrust and squirmed, begging for more with his body.

Alex slammed into Ridley's ass again and again. Jesus, the man was like an addictive drug; the more Alex got, the more he wanted. Without warning, his balls drew up and he was teetering on the edge. With a gasp he reared back, muscles straining, cock twitching and pulsing rapidly deep within Ridley. "Ridley," he said huskily. "Don't you dare fucking move."

Ridley went completely still beneath him as he panted harshly for a few heartbeats. Just when Alex thought he might be able to get himself back under control, Ridley wrapped his legs around Alex's waist, pressed his heels hard against Alex's ass, and thrust up.

"Fuck, fuck. I.... Goddammit, Ridley." He squeezed his eyes shut and gritted his teeth, refusing to let go, to take the last step over the cliff.

Alex thought he would shatter. Ridley was everywhere, surrounding him, and with each breath, each heartbeat, he drew closer to coming. He curled over Ridley and kissed him hard. "Can't.... I have to," he panted against Ridley's lips. "Oh fuck!" He stared into Ridley's eyes while thrusting and rocking, sliding in and out of Ridley's body with no finesse as his orgasm washed over him. He let go, let it sweep him away in pleasure.

Ridley arched hard, rubbing his cock against Alex's flesh. Ridley met each thrust as he held Alex's gaze with heavy lids but he lost the fight to keep them open as he gave in to his own need for release. The tension in his body increased briefly, until his orgasm ripped through him and he cried out Alex's name.

With the last of his strength zapped, Alex collapsed onto Ridley's heaving chest.

He listened to Ridley's heart race; his own was pounding just as fast. They lay there, neither one speaking or moving until their panting breaths slowed. Not wanting to move, but knowing he had to so as not to hurt Ridley, Alex forced himself to shift, groaning with the effort it took. He lay on his side and pulled Ridley to him in a warm embrace. He didn't even care that they were covered in sweat and come, too happy to care as he basked for a bit in his pleasurable high.

Ridley tugged weakly at Alex's hair. "I thought you said I wouldn't be able to come tonight? Such a big ol' softy," Ridley chuckled.

Alex laughed and lifted his head to meet Ridley's teasing gaze. "Softy, huh?" Alex asked and arched a brow. "You just couldn't keep your mouth shut and be happy." He shook his head.

"Oh, I'm ridiculously happy," Ridley said assuredly. "And my ass I'm sure will thank you in the morning—"

Alex placed a finger over Ridley's smiling mouth, silencing him. "I wouldn't take it that far," Alex smirked. "That was just a warm-up." He leaned over, took Ridley's left nipple into his mouth, and bit down on it hard, pulling a yelp from the smug little shit. Satisfied, Alex rolled from the bed and headed to the bathroom.

"Where are you going?" Ridley protested. "I was enjoying that little after-fuck cuddle."

After disposing of the used condom and wiping off, Alex pulled open the cabinet and grabbed a box of condoms and two more bottles of lube. He walked back out into the bedroom with a straight face and dropped the items on Ridley's chest. "Now it's dinner time." He laughed heartily at the look of fear that crossed Ridley's face.

TRUE TO his word, Alex fucked him through the mattress, over the side of the mattress, on the floor, against the wall, and once Alex fucked the sense completely out of him and left him a limp noodle on the bed, he fucked him again. Ridley was pretty sure he passed out the last time when he came, because he remembered Alex slamming into him like a man possessed and the next thing he was aware of was waking up alone in Alex's bed.

Gingerly, Ridley placed his feet on the floor, took a deep breath, and winced as pain shot out from his ass as he stood. Alex had kept his promise: Ridley was definitely questioning the soundness of his taunts as he padded silently across the floor on bare feet.

He didn't bother turning on the light in the bathroom, the moon shining in from the small window enough to make out the porcelain bowl, and quite honestly, Ridley wasn't really sure he was ready to see the damage done to his body. It felt bad enough, his chest, balls, and ass pure fucking fire, the muscles of his limbs sore and knotting up painfully due to some of the positions Alex had put him in. Alex had bent and twisted Ridley like a motherfucking pretzel, and his dumb ass kept begging for more, harder, faster. Ridley shook his head. Yeah, he was a total dumbass, but it had been worth it. At least it had been at the time. Now? Not so much.

He took a piss, then washed his hands and face. Feeling around on the countertop, he found a towel and dried off before tossing it to the floor and going in search of Alex. Ridley may have been sore and walking funny, but he'd put a few impressive marks on Alex. The thought made him grin widely.

Being as quiet as possible in case Alex had gone to sleep on the couch, Ridley made his way into the living room. The couch was empty, as was the lone chair and the floor. The kitchen, too, was empty. He turned in a full circle, searching. The house wasn't that big. There was nowhere Alex could be hiding, no second bedroom.

Movement out the front window caught Ridley's attention, and he cautiously made his way over to it, keeping out of the line of vision of anyone possibly looking in.

In the drive he spotted what appeared to be a dark sedan with its parking lights on. Ridley couldn't make out who was behind the wheel enough to see if it were man or woman, but he recognized the blond head of hair on the man standing outside the car, his arms waving frantically as he spoke.

Ridley couldn't hear what Alex was saying, couldn't even hear a low mumbling sound from this distance, even with the window open slightly. The car engine was also hampering his ability to hear what was being said. However, Ridley could tell by Alex's posture and the way he was pointing and flailing his arms that whatever they were talking about had Alex downright pissed.

Ridley was suddenly on high alert. It could have been nothing more than a heated argument with a shunned lover or an argument with a friend, but given the events of the past week, Ridley was scared for Alex. He debated slipping on some pants and rushing to Alex's side, but hesitated for some unknown reason.

Suddenly Ridley was awash in bright light as the car's headlights came on and the engine roared. Ridley shielded his eyes and watched as the car was thrown into reverse at a fast pace and then the brakes hit, causing the car to spin sideways. The engine roared again and the car lurched forward, sending up gravel as it peeled out of the driveway.

Apparently whatever Alex said had pissed the stranger off as well. Ridley spotted Alex stomping toward the house, and he jerked back from the window. As quickly and as quietly as he could, he rushed to the bedroom, his heart pounding and his breathing more of a pant as adrenaline surged through him. Ridley made a beeline for the bathroom, knowing he wouldn't be able to fake sleep if Alex came in.

Without closing the door all the way to avoid making any noise, Ridley flipped on the light in the bathroom, blinking at the harsh glare, and flushed the toilet. He didn't want Alex to know he'd been spying on him, so he flipped on the water, letting it run as he examined his reflection in the mirror. His hair was pointing in a hundred different directions, the ring in his lip was missing, and his rapidly rising and falling chest was covered in love bites, hickeys, and bruises the exact size of Alex's fingers.

Shockingly, he looked worse, had more marks on his body than he'd had the first time he'd been with Alex. Shaking his head, Ridley cut the water off and flipped the light out as he stepped out of the bathroom. The light was on and Alex was leaning against the doorframe in nothing but a pair of blue sweats, his arms crossed over his chest. He still looked pissed.

"Grab your stuff. I'm taking you home," he informed Ridley.

"Angry ex?" Ridley surmised.

"What?" Alex responded, looking confused.

"I saw you talking to someone out front. The look on your face right now along with your words make me think it's a pissed-off ex."

Alex rolled his eyes. "I wish it were that simple."

When Alex didn't say anything further, Ridley shrugged and pushed past Alex to go in search of his clothes.

He found his jeans and briefs on the floor near the kitchen island and snatched them up. He laid his jeans across the back of the barstool and stepped into his briefs, pulling them up before picking his jeans back up.

"It's not an ex," Alex said again as he joined Ridley in the kitchen. "I can't tell you who it was, but it wasn't an ex."

Ridley shrugged again. He was curious as hell but wasn't going to ask and said as much. "I didn't ask."

Ridley pulled on his jeans, buttoned and zipped them up, and then snatched his T-shirt from the counter and put it on. He was acutely aware of Alex watching him, but he refused to give in to his curiosity. He had a sinking feeling that this would be the last time he saw Alex, and he didn't want his speculation made a reality. Not yet.

After gathering up his shoes and socks, Ridley took them to the couch, shook out his socks and slid them on and then his shoes. He was tying them when Alex joined him on the couch.

"So that's it. You're not going to say anything?"

"What do you want me to say, Alex? You told me to gather up my shit because you were taking me home and that's what I'm doing."

"This…." He waved his hand randomly toward the door. "This isn't about you," he finally settled on.

"Ok." Ridley went to his feet and started to walk toward the door. He'd wait outside for Alex to get dressed and grab his keys. Ridley's heart was pounding painfully and the walls were closing in on him. He needed some fucking air.

"Goddammit, Ridley, stop it," Alex growled angrily. He grabbed on to Ridley's arm and spun him around. "It's not what you think."

"How the fuck do you know what I'm thinking?" Ridley spat, giving Alex a hard glare.

"Because I can see it on your face and you're wrong. This has nothing to do with you."

"Yeah, I fucking believe that," Ridley challenged. "I ended up in the hospital because it has nothing to do with me. I had Kyle so fucking scared of me he nearly pissed himself when he ran into me because it has nothing to do with me, and you're demanding I get dressed in the middle of the night so you can take me home because it has nothing to do with me." Ridley's voice grew with each statement until he was shouting into Alex's face. "You know what? Fuck it, I'll walk."

The flare of anger was so sudden it made his head spin. The uncertainty, the feeling of rejection, the idea of not seeing Alex again, the unanswered questions all came bubbling up and he went with it, let it take him over. It was a hell of a lot better than allowing the sadness below it to creep to the forefront. Ridley yanked his arm from Alex's grip and stomped toward the door. He threw it open and a loud crack sounded, followed by wood on the doorframe going flying. Ridley was tackled and shoved sideways, his shoulder hitting the wall with a painful thud.

"Get down," Alex yelled at the same time he slammed the door shut.

Did someone just try to shoot me? Ridley hesitated, trying to wrap his mind around what the hell had just happened, but he didn't have time.

He flailed as his feet were suddenly knocked from beneath him and he landed on his ass.

"I said get the fuck down. Now stay down and cover your head," Alex spat and went crawling across the floor. He pulled his cell phone from the pocket of his sweats, pushing buttons as he moved. "You led them right to me, you dumb shit. Get back here!" Alex shouted into the phone and then pulled something from between the cushions of the couch, spun, and went to his feet, staying in a low crouch.

Ridley heard the slide of metal against metal the same instant he spotted the gun in Alex's hand. "Stay low to the ground and take cover behind the island," Alex instructed and pointed toward the kitchen.

Another shot rang out and the front porch light went dark. A second shot hit the picture window, shattering it and sending glass flying across the room.

"Go now," Alex snarled as he moved toward the door.

Ridley got moving. On hands and knees he crawled across the floor, rolling into the kitchen as soon as he cleared the entryway and then hiding behind the island. From his vantage point he could see Alex crouched low, hand on the doorknob.

Shit, shit, shit. Ridley had known there was something going on with Alex, something bigger than just a jock's need to pick on a geek, but he hadn't expected this. Someone was shooting at them. "What the fuck, man?" Ridley grumbled under his breath. This wasn't the goddamn Wild West.

"If I go down, you get your ass in my room and call 911. You understand me?" Alex demanded in a loud whisper and tossed the phone to him.

Ridley snagged the cell out of the air. "What the fuck is going on?" Ridley asked, his voice cracking as adrenaline surged through him.

"I said, 'Do you understand me?'" Alex growled.

Ridley nodded.

Alex rolled his shoulders and then eased the gun next to the door and opened it just enough for the barrel to fit through. Wood about a foot above Alex's head splintered as another shot rang out.

"Shit!" Alex grunted and ducked his head as the splinters rained down on him. "Good thing you're a bad shot, asshole!" he yelled out.

Another shot sounded but Ridley didn't see any wood move, and better yet, he didn't see any blood. Alex snorted, a noise sounding suspiciously like a laugh, and then he threw open the door and was gone, the door slamming behind him as he disappeared.

Ridley stared wide-eyed at the spot Alex had just been. He couldn't have just…. Ridley rubbed his hand over his jaw. That crazy fucker went out to confront someone who was shooting at him. *Holy shit, like seriously shooting to take his goddamn head off kind of aiming.*

Ridley had already begun to suspect that Alex wasn't anything like the outward persona he tried to portray. He'd had proof—twice—that sexually Alex was a hell of a lot tougher than Ridley was. Now as he cowered on the floor of the kitchen clutching a cell phone long after the shots ceased, Ridley knew for one hundred percent fact that Alex was a badass motherfucker and Ridley was….

Not.

CHAPTER 12

FROM HIS hiding place on the front porch, Alex worked to slow his rapidly beating heart and harsh breaths. He was fairly certain he'd taken out the shooter and there was either only one intruder or the car barreling down his drive had chased away any accomplices. Alex's effort to calm himself was for nothing, both heart and lungs going wild as the car in the drive came to a stop. Alex jumped up, stormed down the steps, and sprinted across the lawn, meeting the driver as he stepped out of the car.

"Do you see this?" Alex asked, pointing to the wood splinters in his hair. "Do you?"

"Is that wood?" Mick asked and plucked a piece out of Alex's curls and examined it.

"Yes, from the doorframe that shattered over my head. You know, when a bullet was aimed at it." Alex swatted the splinter out of Mick's hand.

"Good thing the guy was a bad shot, eh? I mean seriously, how can anyone miss this mop?" Mick mused and pulled at one of Alex's curls.

"It's not funny! You led them right to me, you dumb shit," Alex accused angrily.

"Whoa now, you can't know it was my fault." Mick gave Alex an exasperated look. "Umm, if they know where you are, do you think it's a good idea to be standing out here in the open bitching at me?"

It took all Alex's effort not to stomp his foot or punch Mick in the face or.... Ugh, the bastard was right. Alex had been so pumped up on adrenaline, as well as pissed off, he'd gone off half-cocked. Recklessly running across the yard to bitch at his friend rather than cautiously assessing his environment was pretty stupid. It wouldn't be the first time Mick had accused him of being crazy. Alex was sure it wouldn't be the last. But regardless of what Mick said, Alex did not have a death wish, more of a slight temper with a short fuse. Maybe he really did need to look into those anger management classes Mick had suggested more than a few times.

"Fine." Alex stabbed a finger in Mick's chest. "But as soon as we deem it safe, I'm reaming your ass."

"I know how badly you want my sexy ass." Mick smirked. "But really? How many times do I have to tell you I don't, nor will I ever, swing your way before you'll give up?"

Alex rolled his eyes. Mick was talking shit, teasing, but he was also taking in his surroundings with a critical eye, focused, listening, watching. He was the levelheaded half of their team.

"I heard the guy scream from over there," Alex informed Mick, pointing at the brush along the side of the house. "Give me your flashlight."

Mick reached into the car and retrieved the light and handed it to Alex. Sweeping the area with a wide beam of light, he headed to where the scream came from, Mick right on his heels. The spot behind the bushes was trampled down, spent casings littered the ground, and there was blood but nothing else.

"Looks like the perp isn't the only one who's a bad shot," Mick commented.

"Hey, at least I hit my target," Alex grumbled and started following the blood trail to the east. The wind still, the nightlife silent in the wake of the disturbance, the only sound was the low rumble of Mick's idling engine. The trail led them to an opening on the other side of a small grove of trees and ended next to tire tracks.

"Shit," Alex complained and rubbed at the ache that had settled at the back of his neck. "Did you see any other cars when you came in?"

Mick shook his head and pulled out his cell. "I gotta call this in."

"Goddammit," Alex cursed again. "I am so sick of this bullshit."

"Oh, quit your bitching. You hated working at the library. Here's your chance to get a manlier job."

"I got your manly"—Alex growled and grabbed his crotch—"right here."

Mick laughed, then into his cell said, "Ramirez here. We've been compromised. He's gotten himself found out." Mick arched a brow at Alex. "Again."

Alex flipped him off.

He'd hated this place since day one. Hated the school and the job and who the hell in their right mind would want to live in the northern peninsula of Michigan anyway, especially in the winter. And they thought he was crazy. Crazy was being a goddamn Yooper. The only thing that had made Slater even slightly tolerable was Ridley.

"Oh fuck. Ridley!"

Alex took off at a dead run.

"Hey, where the hell are you going?" Mick yelled out.

Alex ignored him. Christ, how had he forgotten Ridley, the one good thing in his life lately? He was the one person who had made the loneliness of anonymity tolerable. Alex sprinted across the yard, bound up the stairs, and threw open the door.

"Ridley!"

"I'm here," Ridley called out from the kitchen.

Alex halted next to the island, heart pounding so hard it caused a rush of blood to drown out all sound. But Ridley was there, sitting with his back against the cabinets, knees up with his arms wrapped around them, and looking a little freaked out, but safe and whole.

Relieved, Alex fell to his knees next to him. "You okay?" he asked and ran a hand along Ridley's cheek.

"What the hell just happened?" Ridley asked sounding shell-shocked, eyes wide.

"Is he okay?" Mick asked as he barreled into the kitchen and slammed into the counter. Mick Ramirez was a big man, standing well over six foot and tipping the scales at a meaty two-fifty. There wasn't an ounce of fat on the man, so when he hit something—the counter—it made a hell of a sound. With his dark hair shaved close and a large scar along his olive-colored skin from chin to temple, he was an imposing son of a bitch, and Alex completely understood why Ridley tensed, the freaked-out expression on his face morphing into full-on fear.

"It's okay," Alex said soothingly, the need to comfort automatic. He sighed heavily when he suddenly realized what he was doing, what he was thinking, what Ridley was beginning to mean to him. He slid his hand down to squeeze Ridley's shoulder reassuringly. "You're okay."

"Who—" Ridley's voice cracked and he cleared his throat. "Who is that?" he asked with a frown, nodding toward Mick.

"Ramirez," Alex answered and turned to look up at his partner. Mick wasn't really his partner in the typical sense of the word, but since Mick had been assigned as Alex's protector, the term was fitting. "He *used* to be my best friend. He only looks like a hardass, but he's a big ol' pussy cat."

"Hey, Ridley, call me Mick. Glad you're okay." Mick then looked at Alex and rolled his eyes dramatically. "I got to make some arrangements to get your ass out of this mess. Yell if you need me."

Alex gave a curt nod and then turned his attentions back to Ridley, who was staring at Alex's side, his eyes impossibly wide. Alex looked down and realized he still had his gun in his hand. He set it aside and cupped Ridley's chin, forcing him to look up and meet his gaze.

"You...." Ridley shook his head. "There were bullets and... glass exploding... and... and.... What the fuck is wrong with you?" Ridley snapped and surged to his feet, causing Alex to flail and land on his ass. Ridley put his hands on his hips and scowled down at him. "When bullets are flying, you don't run directly into their path. What the hell were you thinking? They were shooting at us. And you... you...." Ridley threw up his hands in obvious frustration. "Who the hell does that?"

Alex pulled himself to a sitting position, picked up his gun, and went to his feet, wincing as pain shot through his right one. He set the gun on the counter and lifted his foot—a large piece of wood was imbedded into the heel. Now that the adrenaline rush was seeping from his body, the effects of running over brush and rocks on bare feet were making themselves painfully known.

"Oh shit, you're bleeding," Ridley muttered, concern changing the angry tone of his voice.

"I'm fine." Alex shrugged and jumped up to sit on the counter, then laid his foot across his thigh. "You mind handing me a towel?" The piece of wood wasn't much bigger in diameter than a toothpick, but the way it was throbbing, it felt like the whole fucking tree.

Ridley grabbed one from the handle on the stove and brought it to him. "You got a first aid kit? Maybe some disinfectant?" Ridley asked as he stared down at the wound.

"Under the sink in the bathroom."

Ridley left the room and Alex gritted his teeth, grabbed the stick, and yanked. "Son of a bitch," he hissed and pressed the towel against his foot to stop the flow of blood from the numerous cuts. He examined the other foot; there were a few scrapes, what looked like small slivers of debris along the ball of his foot and in his heel, but none were actively bleeding.

Clean towels and first aid kit in hand, Ridley came back into the room and silently laid out his supplies next to Alex. Ridley lifted the towel from Alex's foot, examined the wounds, and poked at the oozing ones.

Alex flinched and grimaced but didn't complain. He watched Ridley carefully as he cleaned the wounds, a thoughtful expression on his face. Alex didn't say a word. Ridley was handling the shock fairly well at the moment and was undoubtedly trying to process it all.

Once the wounds were clean and dry, Ridley wrapped Alex's foot in gauze and taped it in place. "Thanks," Alex said sincerely.

Ridley simply nodded and then gathered up the dirty towels and first aid kit and left the room once again without a word.

Alex ran a hand through his curls, his fingers tangling in the tousled strands, bits of wood falling free. On the bright side, he'd be getting a new look and the crazy mop would be the first thing to go. The possibility of a haircut was the only good thing about this whole fucked-up situation. He huffed out a breath and then gingerly got down from the counter. He went to the cabinet and pulled out a can of coffee—he'd no doubt need the caffeine. It was going to be a long day. God only knew where he'd be moving to, but first he had a shit-ton of explaining to do.

He just hoped Ridley would forgive him for all the lies.

RIDLEY RESTED his hands on the vanity and studied his haunted reflection in the mirror. For the second time since he'd awakened, he found himself hiding in the bathroom. "Holy shit," he mumbled to his stunned reflection. He'd suspected there was a lot more to Alex, but he didn't expect bullets and windows exploding and... big scary Mexicans with a bad suit and gun. He also damn sure didn't expect to be sitting on a kitchen floor scared shitless. Now he knew what that look on Kyle's face had been. Utter fucking fear. Not only did he know what it looked like, he now knew exactly what it felt like.

"He went right out into the line of fire," Ridley muttered incredulously. *Right out the goddamn door. Into the path of bullets!* Alex could have been killed. Jesus! Ridley was going to be sick.

Gut roiling and bile burning his throat, he plopped his ass down on the commode and put his head between his legs. Oh how familiar this position felt. Obviously one of the side effects of hanging with Alex Firestone—if that was even his damn name.

Sad thing was, he didn't know which bothered him more: the fact that Alex wasn't some cute, mild-mannered librarian but instead a crazy fucker who could beat five men down and wasn't a stranger to a gun, or his own reaction to the threats. Both times he'd been completely useless. The first time he'd gotten himself bonked on the head and knocked out, and this time he'd cowered like a scared little girl watching a horror film—minus the screaming. He'd been too damn scared to scream.

Ridley shook his head and then hung it in his hands. What a loser.

Not as big of a loser as someone hiding in a bathroom about ready to puke. True. He had to get his shit together. A few deep breaths to steady himself and he pushed up to his feet. He turned on the faucet, splashed some cold water on his face, and then rinsed out his mouth. Neither made him feel any better, but it was time to pull up his big-boy pants and get the answers he so desperately needed. There was the very real possibility that he was falling in love with a criminal and he wasn't sure how he felt about that.

Love.

Ridley stumbled back in horror. He wasn't in love with a criminal. No way could he be in love. Lust maybe, but…. Ridley blew out a long, relieved breath. Yeah, that had to be it. He enjoyed the fucking with Alex. The man intrigued him like no one ever, and yeah, he liked spending time with him. Liked hearing him laugh and seeing him smile and the way his body fit against his own. He got off on the little hint of danger he'd catch sight of in Alex, really liked the fucking, and the man was super hot. Ridley nodded to his reflection. "Did I mention I really like the fucking?" he mouthed silently and then winked.

Yeah, he was in lust and being in lust with a criminal was nowhere near as bad as being in love with a criminal. Or being in love period. The thought made him shudder.

CHAPTER 13

"THERE'S COFFEE in the pot." Alex nodded toward the counter from where he sat with his own mug.

"How's he doing?" Mick asked.

"I don't know. He doctored my feet up—"

"Your feet," Mick interrupted, one brow raised.

Alex lifted his bandaged foot. "I got a sliver."

"Pussy," Mick chuckled and took a seat across from him.

"Shut up," Alex grumbled over the rim of his cup.

"So...."

"He's been in the bathroom since," Alex responded, knowing what Mick was asking. "I was about to go beat on the door when I heard the shower come on. I think he's a bit freaked out."

"Ya think?" Mick asked smartly. "I'm sure it's not every day he's banging some dude and it ends in a gun fight."

"We weren't banging," Alex shot back and shifted in his seat uncomfortably. "That was earlier," he muttered.

"You're such a slut," Mick chuckled.

Mick was the FBI agent that had given a lecture on criminal profiling when Alex was at the academy. He was eight years older than Alex, but from that moment on he and Mick had become fast friends. Alex didn't go around advertising the fact that he was gay, but he'd never denied it either. Mick, claiming he had a high-tech gaydar system, had tried to set Alex up with his brother not long after they met. Alex was far from a slut, but if Mick knew some of the wild times Alex and Mick's little brother had, he'd think Alex was one instead of only teasing him about it. The thought made him grin, but then he glared at his partner.

"Hey, kiss my ass," Alex grumbled. "I've been stuck in this hick town for a year. A man has needs."

"Aww, poor baby," Mick muttered sarcastically.

"Besides, my sex life, just like your ass, is totally off limits. That is, unless you've changed your mind?" Alex asked, intentionally dropping his voice to a low and seductive tone.

"If I did, I certainly wouldn't be giving it up to you."

"Ooh, so you *have* been thinking about it."

"Don't make me beat you," Mick huffed at him.

Alex laughed at the way Mick's nose wrinkled. Mick may have been totally cool with Alex's sexuality, but the idea of sucking dick or taking it up the ass always made him a bit squeamish. Alex totally understood his aversion since the thought of sticking his face in a va-jay-jay always made him a little grossed out too.

"So what have you found out?" Alex asked, turning the conversation to a more serious matter.

"Not a whole lot," Mick admitted and pulled out a small notebook from his pocket and flipped it open. "We've checked all the local hospitals and after-hours emergency care facilities and no gunshots. The hit our guy took either wasn't serious or he's lying dead somewhere."

"Any thoughts on how they found me?" Alex asked as he shifted in his chair to prop his bum foot up.

"No. But don't you find it highly suspect that right after you have to identify yourself after your little brawl, you end up with a visitor?"

"You think it's an inside job?"

"That would be my guess," Mick responded with a shrug.

"That just doesn't make sense. I know Gutierrez has a hell of a reach, but seriously, in podunk Slater?"

"If you have a better explanation, I'm all ears," Mick responded with a hint of challenge in his dark eyes.

Alex scrubbed a hand over his face and pinched the bridge of his nose. Mick, of course, was right; it was the only explanation. "So what now?" he asked tiredly.

"We have a team setting up a perimeter around your place and as soon as the details are worked out, we move you."

"I'm getting so fucking tired of this. I have half a damn mind to say screw it and go home. Take my chances."

"You'll get yourself killed. Just be patient a little longer."

"First it was six months, then a year. It's been one delay after another. How much longer am I expected to wait? I'm going fucking stir-crazy!"

"You've always been stir-crazy." Mick grinned crookedly.

"Yeah well, now I'm stir-crazy and have no one to take my frustrations out on or shoot."

"I bet the guy who left blood all over your bushes would beg to differ."

That pulled a small smile from Alex. It shouldn't feel good to know he'd put a bullet in another man, but it did. Besides, the son of a bitch was shooting at him first; bastard deserved it.

"All right, I'll wait a bit longer," Alex finally agreed with a long-suffering sigh. "But I want somewhere warm. And a beach."

"I'll see what I can do. What about Ridley?"

Alex froze, his mug halfway to his mouth. "What about him?"

"How much does he know?" Mick inquired.

"Not a thing." Alex set his coffee aside. "I wasn't that lonely that I started crying on his shoulders about the injustice of it all. Sheesh, give me a little credit."

"That's not what I meant." The patient irritation was clear in his voice. "Ridley was with you during your alley brawl and again tonight at the OK Corral. They may have already IDed him."

"Ah, shit." Alex drummed his fingers on the countertop. The idea that he may have put Ridley in danger, that these assholes would hurt him to get to Alex made him want to commit murder. He'd just have to make damn sure no one got the chance. "Okay, how about this? I'll keep him with me until we know if he's been IDed."

"And if he has been?" Mick asked cautiously, as if he was worried how Alex would respond.

"Then I take him with me," Alex said without hesitation.

"You know that's not how it works. We don't have the authorization to make that call. But I can assure you—"

"I don't care how this works," Alex interrupted. "I got him into this mess. I give no fucks about policy or authorization or whatever. I'm telling you right now, if it comes down to it, Ridley's going with me."

"Where am I going?"

Alex spun around to find Ridley coming out of the bathroom, running a towel over his damp hair. "Well... um... you see," Alex sputtered and then huffed out a frustrated breath. He waved toward the coffee maker. "You might want to grab a cup of coffee and take a seat for this."

"That bad, huh?" Ridley commented.

"Maybe. Depends on how you look at it," Alex said without elaborating.

"Well, the way I look at it is when people go around shooting at me, I'd say that's pretty bad," Ridley pointed out as he grabbed a cup from the hook and poured himself a cup of coffee.

Alex shot a look at Mick, who was looking back and forth between him and Ridley with a hint of amusement. Mick downed the rest of his coffee and then stood. "I've got a few more calls I need to make," he announced. "I'll leave you two to talk."

"Traitor," Alex mouthed as Mick walked by. His partner's only response was to blow Alex a kiss. He really needed to pick better friends.

RIDLEY ADDED a little cream and sugar to his coffee. The shower had done a world of good to calm him and gave him time to get his shit together. He'd given himself a little pep talk while standing under the hot spray, convincing himself it was quite normal to be a little nuts when one has bullets whizzing by their head for the first time.

He took the seat across from Alex, rolled his shoulders, and then jumped right in to the conversation. "Okay, let's hear it."

"I'm not sure how much I can tell you."

"How about we start with, oh I don't know... everything."

"Everything?" Alex asked with a tilt of his head.

"Yeah, and don't try pumping sunshine up my ass or sugarcoating it," Ridley warned. "I'm really not in the mood for any more surprises or bullshit tonight—" He cut his gaze toward the window, the sun just beginning to rise. "—this morning, whatever, man."

Alex stared at Ridley for a long moment. He cleared his throat and licked his lips nervously. "I can't tell you everything. It's classified."

Ridley gave Alex a once-over. Alex still hadn't put on a shirt. Although he'd seen Alex's body before—hell, he'd licked, kissed, and groped nearly every inch of it—given the turn of events he was seeing it in a new light. The puzzle pieces started to shift into place. Alex was fit, really fit. *Click.* Good with a gun. *Click.* Had a partner. *Click, click.* Said shit like *classified, authority,* and *policy.*

Click. Click. Click. A nearly complete puzzle with only a couple pieces missing.

"I've already figured you're either an undercover cop or a Fed, and whoever was shooting up the place damn sure wasn't here for some poor ass mechanical engineering student. Furthermore, whoever sent said shooter/shooters probably knew I was here or if they didn't they do now and probably think I'm part of... whatever it is you're involved in, and now I'm in danger." He picked up his mug and took a sip and looked at Alex over the rim. "How am I doing?"

Alex leaned back in his chair, his arms crossed over his chest, and grinned. "Impressive," he said wryly.

"So I ask again, what mess and where are we going?"

Alex continued to stare at Ridley with a shit-eating grin, but after a few seconds, he sighed heavily and sat forward, leaning his forearms on the counter and wrapping his hands around his mug. Alex didn't look at him while he spoke but rather kept his head down. "I'm not a Fed, nor am I undercover, but I am a cop."

"Well that's better than fucking a criminal, I suppose," Ridley responded in amusement. "I guess it could be useful if I ever get a ticket."

Alex snorted in response. "Sorry, bud, you're on your own with the locals. I got no pull. Actually, I officially don't exist, and Alex the library assistant can't do shit to get you out of your traffic woes."

"Is Alex even your real name?"

"Yeah," he answered with a curt nod and then looked up at Ridley from beneath his long lashes, his lip curling into a sly grin. "But I stole the name Firestone from a porn star I had the hots for when I was younger."

Ridley snickered. "Nice," he said approvingly.

"Thanks."

"So you're a cop pretending to be a library assistant and you like to borrow names from porn stars. Neither of which, I might point out, explains why there was someone shooting at us tonight. So if you're not undercover, what are you and why does someone want you dead?"

"I'm going to need more caffeine for this," Alex mused and started to rise.

"I got it," Ridley offered as he pushed out of his chair. "You talk." He headed to retrieve the coffee pot.

"I was serious when I said it was classified," Alex said sincerely. "And trust me when I tell you, some things you're better off not knowing, but I'll tell you as much as I can."

"Fair enough," Ridley conceded as he refilled Alex's mug and then topped off his own.

"I was a couple years out of the academy. Had this crazy notion that I was going to change the world one bad guy at a time. I was ambitious, cocky, and confident."

"Was?" Ridley asked with a little snicker as he brought the sugar and cream back to the counter and took a seat.

"Yeah." Alex looked up at Ridley, his coffee cup stopping midway to his mouth as he smiled slowly. "Okay, I may still be a bit of all three," he agreed and then blew into his mug past a sly grin.

Satisfied, Ridley leaned back in his chair. "Please continue."

Alex shrugged, took a gulp of the caffeine he claimed he so desperately needed, and then nodded, picking up where he'd left off. "I was on the graveyard shift and one night my partner and I stopped at a gas station just out of town—"

"What town?" Ridley interrupted.

"That's one of those need-to-knows," Alex said, shaking his head. "My partner went in to grab us some coffees and I went to take a piss. The bathroom was locked so I stepped behind the building." Alex took another healthy gulp and then leaned back with an audible sigh. "Long story short, I stumbled upon something the players never intended the law to see, and I found myself the star witness for the prosecuting attorney."

"What did you see?" Ridley asked curiously. Alex held Ridley's gaze, an almost apologetic glint in his blue eyes. "Another one of those classified things, huh?" Ridley answered for him.

"Yes," Alex answered curtly.

"Okay. So you saw something you're not supposed to see. Got it, but cops testify all the time in criminal cases. It doesn't explain why you're dressing like a geek and working in a library for the last—" Ridley ticked off the months on his fingers. "—at least eight months."

"A year and a half," Alex corrected. "And it makes perfect sense when the information you have can help bring down one of the most wanted and most dangerous drug cartels."

Click. The last piece of the puzzle slid smoothly into place.

"Witness protection," Ridley muttered and then whistled low. "Now it makes perfect sense."

"Yeah, well, knowing doesn't make it any safer for you. If you weren't such a persistent little shit, you wouldn't be in this fucking mess," Alex grumbled.

"I didn't hear you complaining last night. At least not until you woke up." Ridley lifted his shirt and looked down at the numerous marks on his torso, then back up at Alex with a seductive curl of his lip. "I obviously like living on the edge of danger."

Alex ran his gaze leisurely down Ridley's body, a satisfied grin on his face. "Danger looks good on you," he remarked and licked his lips. Alex then jerked his gaze up to meet Ridley's and waved a hand at him. "Cover that up, this is serious."

Ridley chuckled and did as Alex asked, but Alex wasn't the only one feeling a bit of pride. The look of lust in the man's eyes before Alex visibly had to push it away was all Ridley needed to know. "Sorry," he responded, not feeling the least bit apologetic. "I'm not making light of the situation, honest I'm not. Waking up and finding out how badly you handle being shot at is a sobering event, and in all honesty, I hope to God I never have to discover if I would handle it any better a second time."

"I'm hoping like hell you don't have to find out either and that they haven't figured out who you are. Better yet, hopefully they weren't even aware of you being here. I've got Mick looking into it. But until we know, you're staying here, which means unfortunately you may just have to find out how you'll do. These people have no issue taking out cops, Feds, or goddamn politicians," Alex spat angrily and clenched his fists. "To them you're nothing more than an irritation. Something to be disposed of."

"And if they don't know about me?"

"Then you can go back to your quiet life as a college student at Slater University and no one in this sleepy little town ever need know."

"And you?" Ridley asked cautiously.

"I slip away under the cover of darkness and Alex Firestone ceases to exist," Alex said matter-of-factly.

Ridley's gut flip-flopped sickeningly in reaction to the thought of Alex leaving and Ridley not knowing where he'd gone, if he was okay, or if he'd ever see him again. Since he didn't know where Alex was from or even what his last name was, the chances he'd be able to find him again were slim to none. Ridley found himself actually hoping whoever was after Alex knew about him. Yeah, it meant he'd be in danger and yet it didn't seem as awful a possibility as losing Alex.

"What's that look for?" Alex asked, pulling Ridley out of his musings.

"Huh?" He blinked a few times, trying to push down the uneasiness and get back into the conversation.

"That look right there," Alex offered and pointed a finger at Ridley. "It looks like your dog just ran away or something."

Ridley waved him off without commenting on Alex's observation, instead turning the conversation back to the more immediate concerns. "So what do we do now?"

"We wait," Alex responded curtly. "Until we know what we're dealing with and how much they know, we sit tight. But I need you to understand the severity of this situation, Ridley. From here on out, until I either plop you back into university life or take you with me, you do everything I say without question. Got it?"

"Got it," Ridley agreed.

"I mean it," Alex reiterated. "If we leave, you leave everything behind. Even your family won't know what happened to you. Are you prepared for that?"

His heart was pounding so hard Ridley could only nod. He was already feeling guilty as hell for hoping he'd be going with Alex, knowing what it would do to his mom and dad. Even knowing how scared and heartbroken they'd be, what his disappearance would do to Rae, Ridley couldn't help the way he felt.

CHAPTER 14

STARING OUT into the dark, Alex leaned his forehead against the window; the cool glass against his heated flesh caused him to shiver. Although he couldn't see them, he knew at least thirty heavily armed and highly trained men surrounded his small home, and yet he still didn't feel completely safe. He'd been an idiot to fall into a false sense of security. He'd been an even bigger fool to let his guard down and allow someone to get close to him. One was never safe from Gutierrez, and now he'd brought Ridley into the shit storm.

He'd already told Ridley too much, and yet it bothered him that he couldn't tell him more. He needed Ridley to truly understand how serious the situation was, how dangerous it was. However, he knew if he told him any more than he already had, Ridley could potentially be in even more danger. Totally unacceptable.

What he really wanted to do was snatch Ridley up and run. The waiting was driving him nuts. Funny, since that was all he'd pretty much been doing for the last year and a half. Waiting. With one tactical delay after another, Gutierrez's attorney had been able to use the system to keep his client out of the courtroom. He hadn't been able to keep Gutierrez out of jail, but that mattered little. The drug lord was able to conduct his business, arrange his hits, and continue to fund his empire, all from his six by nine concrete and metal home, without missing a beat. There was no telling how long the wait would be, but in the grand scheme of things, did it matter? When Gutierrez's case went to trial, after Alex testified, even if the man was convicted, imprisoned, and the key thrown away, Alex could never return to his old life. He would forever be looking over his shoulder.

He squeezed his eyes shut as a wave of remorse washed over him, causing him to tremble. Everyone he'd ever loved, his mom, dad, little sister, grandparents, and scores of close friends had no clue what had happened to him. Literally within hours of watching Gutierrez swing the fatal blow, Alex Castren had been MIA. Alex understood why it had to be this way, but it didn't help to ease the heaviness in his heart when he thought of what his loved ones must have gone through. What they continued to endure each day. He'd never be able to be a part of their lives again, but he held on to the notion that, hopefully, once the trial was over, they'd know what had happened to him and that he wasn't dead. Would it ease their pain? Perhaps a little. Would it make it better knowing? Doubtful.

"Hey, Alex, how you holding up?" Mick asked as he entered Alex's bedroom and leaned against the wall near the window.

Alex looked over at his partner with tired eyes. "I've had my fill of waiting for the day. You got anything to change that?"

Mick pursed his lips and nodded. Alex could tell from the guarded expression on Mick's face that he wasn't going to like what he was about to hear.

"We picked up one of Gutierrez's men....," Mick said warily.

When his partner didn't comment further, Alex snapped. "Just spit it out!" The stresses of the past eighteen hours were catching up with him, and he was in no mood for evasiveness.

"Going in to Ridley's apartment," Mick responded with true regret and winced.

"Son of a motherfucking monkey," Alex ground out angrily. Alex curled his hands into fists as he struggled to rein in his temper. The urge to lash out was huge and he turned away from the window before another one got shattered.

"You knew there was a high probability they'd know about Ridley," Mick reminded him. He kept his voice low and even as if speaking with a wild animal.

"Is that supposed to be your attempt at making me feel better about this, because I gotta tell ya, Mick, it sucks," Alex grumbled, stomping his feet as he began to pace. He needed to get a grip on his anger, as he was on the verge of committing homicide. "I need a drink or a smoke or.... I don't fucking know what I need, but I need something."

Mick, ignoring Alex's temper tantrum, stepped up in front of him and tapped a smoke out of his pack and held it out to Alex. "It's all I got, man," he offered with a shrug.

Alex took it and slipped it between his lips. Mick struck a match and lit it for him. Alex took a long drag and blew it out slowly. He rarely smoked. It wasn't that he didn't enjoy it, he did, but he hated the stink it left behind. Not to mention it wasn't good for his health, but neither was being chased by a homicidal drug lord. He took another long drag.

Mick didn't say a word, giving Alex time to calm down as he finished his smoke. Mick was used to Alex's temper, and while he could be a real asshole at times, Mick knew it was never directed at him, but rather the situation. Alex had witnessed Mick's impressive temper before and never took the colorful things that came out of Mick's mouth when he was raging, personal. It was part of what made them good friends. They understood each other.

Alex finished his cigarette and dropped the butt into the commode. Wrinkling his nose at the smell, he washed his hands before rejoining Mick in the bedroom, feeling only marginally calmer.

Mick was sitting on the edge of the bed staring down at his hands. He looked up as Alex walked in. "Feeling better?"

"Not really," he grunted and sat down next to him. "The worst part is I only have myself to blame. I'm the one who brought him into this."

"You know assigning blame isn't going to do a fucking thing," Mick said. "It is what it is, and instead of sitting around punishing yourself, we need to get you packed and on the road."

"Don't you mean us?"

"Your request was denied, but—"

"I don't give a fuck whether it was approved or not," Alex snarled and pushed to his feet. "I told you I'm not going anywhere without him, and I damn well meant it." Alex glared down at his partner.

Mick tilted his head and looked at Alex with an exasperated expression. "And if you would shut the fuck up and stop interrupting me, you would have heard the rest of what I had to say."

Alex ran his hands through his hair, staring up at the ceiling as he blew out an angry breath. "All right, let me hear it."

"I'll be lucky if I don't get fired or, worse, thrown in jail, but I disagree with the director and think the safest place for Ridley is with you." Mick went to his feet and looked at Alex pointedly with a crooked grin. "I like to think I'm protecting the good folks of Louisiana who have to live near you if you're not allowed to take your little playmate with you."

"He's not a playmate...." Alex chuckled, instantly feeling better. "Well, all right, he kind of is. And we're going to play in Louisiana?" Alex asked excitedly. "I love New Orleans."

"It's not exactly New Orleans," Mick muttered barely loud enough for Alex to hear as he pushed past him.

Alex frowned. "I know that tone," he accused, following after Mick.

"Let's just enjoy your happy mood for a moment, shall we, hmm?" Mick tossed over his shoulder.

"Sounds ominous," Alex complained.

"Shh," Mick hummed and nodded toward the couch. "You'll wake him up."

Alex glared at his smugly grinning partner, but he didn't push the point. Not yet anyway. Instead he went to the cabinet and pulled out a couple glasses and the nearly empty bottle of bourbon and brought them to the counter. He filled each glass with two fingers of the amber fluid and handed one to Mick.

"When do we head out?" he asked in a hushed voice.

Mick glanced down at his watch. "About an hour."

"That doesn't give me much time to prepare him," he muttered and swirled the liquid in his glass before throwing it back and drinking it down in one gulp.

"That's probably for the best," Mick pointed out. He glanced back to where Ridley was curled up on the couch, just the top of his head peeking out from beneath the throw blanket. "I mean really, how do you prepare someone for something like this?"

Alex's chest tightened painfully as he remembered what it had felt like the first time he was whisked off to a safe house. He poured another healthy shot. You really couldn't prepare anyone for leaving everything and everyone you know and love behind. He rolled his neck, the tension beginning to cause a painful throb at the base of his skull, and looked down at his drink. "Am I driving?" he asked without looking up.

"No."

"Good." Alex threw back the other shot, grimacing as it burned all the way down to his churning gut.

Mick pushed his bourbon across the counter without taking a sip. "I'm going to go talk to the team leader." He looked at Alex morosely. "We pull out in an hour."

Alex laid his hands flat on the counter and hung his head. One hour. Not much time to pack up his belongings and tell a man his life was about to be completely turned upside down and inside out. He shook his head.

"Fucking Gutierrez," he muttered under his breath. If he ever got the chance to get his hands on the bastard, he'd show him what it felt like to be turned inside out.

RIDLEY OPENED his eyes, blinking rapidly as he tried to figure out where he was, but it was too dark and his brain hadn't quite woken up yet.

"Ridley."

He jerked upright at the sound of his name, the blanket falling away.

"Hey, hey. It's just me." Alex laid a hand on Ridley's calf, grounding him.

"Jesus," he muttered sleepily and rubbed at his burning eyes. "I was having a hell of a dream."

"A good one?"

Ridley tried to remember, but the details of the dream were elusive. The only thing he remembered was feeling incredibly happy. "I think so." He raised his arms up over his head, arching his back, stretching as he yawned. When he was finally able to focus on Alex's face where he was sitting at the opposite end of the sofa, staring at him, the sadness in his blue eyes caused Ridley's heart to skip a beat.

"What is it?" he asked in alarm, shoving the covers off and planting his feet on the floor.

"I'm sorry, Ridley. I wish...." Alex pursed his lips and shook his head, the sadness flaring brightly into anger. "One of the men hunting me was spotted at your apartment."

Ridley moved to sit next to Alex and laid his hand on Alex's thigh, stroking it in an attempt to soothe. "I've thought about it a lot since you first told me and was pretty much expecting this news. Does it suck? Hell yeah and I really don't want to think about what this is going to do to my family and friends. But it is what it is, right?"

Alex sniffed and laid his hand over Ridley's and gave it a squeeze. "Funny, Mick said the same thing. And you're both right, we're all just going to have to deal with it, but I don't have to like it. I also won't stop regretting putting you in danger. I can only promise that I'll do everything in my power to keep you safe."

A snort of laughter escaped Ridley, and he coughed into his hand to try and cover it up. Obviously he hadn't been all that successful judging by the strange look Alex shot at him. "Sorry, I'm not laughing at you or at the situation. But damn, is this a complete one-eighty."

"What do you mean?"

"All the times I thought I needed to be the tough guy and protect you from the likes of Kyle Bouche. Now, knowing what I do about you...." He snorted again. "I find it hilarious is all."

"Don't get too comfortable with giving up your superhero persona just yet. We're going to have to watch each other's back until this mess is over." He leaned over and pecked Ridley's cheek. "But, I'm glad you can still laugh."

Ridley cupped the back of Alex's head before he could pull away and pressed his mouth against Alex's. "Laughing's not the only thing I can do to show my enjoyment," he stated and swiped the tip of his tongue across Alex's bottom lip.

"Really?" Alex asked, a cocky grin curling his mouth. "I'd have thought after last night...." He arched a brow, the meaning obvious without further need for words.

"Yeah, well.... So when do we leave?" Ridley asked dubiously, quickly changing the subject before he started thinking about just what Alex had done to him to create the soreness in his backside and the soreness in other areas.

"Within the hour."

"Oh shit," Ridley huffed and jumped to his feet. "That doesn't give me much time to pack. You better run me to my place."

"Ridley," Alex said and grabbed onto Ridley's arm before he could move too far away.

"Yeah," he responded distractedly, already thinking about what needed to go and what could stay.

"You can't go back to your place."

"What?" Ridley asked in confusion and tried to shrug out of Alex's grip. "I've got to grab my stuff."

Alex refused to release him. "I'm sorry. I can't let you go back to your place and I can't allow you to get your stuff."

"What? Why?" Ridley stared blankly at Alex, still not understanding why he couldn't spend a few minutes to throw his belongings into a bag, at the very least clean underwear and his laptop.

"First of all, it's not safe," Alex informed him. "Secondly, we can't tip anyone off that you're leaving. Mick will make sure your place isn't disturbed by anyone until your family comes to retrieve your belongings."

The full scope of what was happening came rushing down on Ridley like a ton of bricks and staying standing on shaking legs took serious effort. "Oh" was all he could push out past his constricted throat.

Ridley blinked back the tears that burned his eyes as Alex slowly slid his arms around him and hugged him. "It's going to be okay," Alex whispered. "I promise."

Ridley closed his eyes and nodded slowly, resting his chin on Alex's shoulder. Ridley wasn't worried about himself; he just hoped his parents would be okay and that, once this was all over, Rae would forgive him.

CHAPTER 15

"HACKBERRY? ARE you fucking kidding me? And what the hell is that smell?" Alex complained, wrinkling his nose in disgust at the horrible odor.

"Sorry, sir, I don't pick the destination, simply drive the car," Agent Daigle said as he set Alex's bags on the floor near the door. "And I believe it's sulfur you smell, sir."

"You mean you can smell the town all the way down here?" Alex asked incredulously. "And stop calling me sir. That would be my grandpa."

"Yeah, the process of mining sulfur requires pumping hot steam into the ground, liquidizing the mineral, and pumping the liquid to the surface. So if the wind is blowing in the right direction, you're going to smell it from miles away," Ridley offered as he draped an arm over Alex's shoulders. "You'll get used to it."

"And how in the hell do you know this?" Alex asked as he looked over at Ridley with a hard glare.

"Some of us actually went to college. You know, to learn."

"Ha-ha. You're such a funny man," Alex said sarcastically, but he couldn't help but laugh at the goofy smile on Ridley's face.

Ridley had taken everything in stride. Being whisked away in the middle of the night, transferred from car to car, a flight on a scary-ass ancient plane, and still more car rides, he hadn't complained once. He hadn't asked questions and kept a smile on his face the entire time. Alex was beginning to think Ridley was either a really happy person or totally fucking insane. The jury was still out, but he was beginning to lean more toward the latter.

"You'll find the house stocked with everything you need. I suggest starting with the desk in the office," Agent Daigle informed them and pulled an envelope from the inside pocket of his suit jacket and handed it to Alex. "Your identifications, sir."

Alex started to complain about being called sir again but figured it wasn't worth it and took the envelope. "Thanks."

Agent Daigle nodded to them and was gone.

"So who are we?" Ridley asked, sounding like a kid on Christmas morning.

Alex opened the envelope and pulled out the contents. He studied the first ID, a Louisiana driver's license with Ridley's picture. "You are now officially Ridley Richmond." He handed the ID to Ridley, as well as a birth certificate and social security card.

"It's got a certain ring to it, doesn't it?" Ridley chuckled.

Alex then checked out his documents and frowned. "Ridley, let me see your birth certificate."

"Why, what's wrong?" he asked as he handed it over.

Alex dropped the other stuff on the dining room table and compared the two certificates side by side. "That asshole! I am so going to fucking kill him."

"Who?"

"Mick," Alex growled and shoved the papers at Ridley. "Look who our parents are."

Ridley scanned them, his eyes widening in shock as he read. "Brothers?" He then burst out laughing.

"It's not funny. Just wait till I get my hands on him."

Ridley continued to laugh uncontrollably. "Sorry," he got out between giggles.

Alex snatched the documents out of the cackling man's hands and shoved everything back into the envelope.

"Oh come on, you ol' sour puss," Ridley snickered and poked Alex in the ribs. "You have to admit it's pretty funny."

Alex rolled his eyes but he couldn't help but laugh at Ridley. Yeah, it was a little funny. Still not as funny as the time Alex had hacked into

Mick's computer and changed his background photo. Mick had opened it up to show their buddy Carlton photos of his new Harley; instead Carlton got an eyeful of some hot man-on-man action.

"Yeah, whatever," he conceded, hiding his grin. "We'll see how funny you think it is when you're wanting a little something, something. 'Cause I'm thinking there aren't a whole lot of opportunities here in the big ol' town of Hackberry."

"Why would I need to go looking when I got you?"

"Oh hell no," Alex hooted. "There will be no incest going down in this house. That's just...." He scrunched up his nose and shook his hands. "Eww."

"I don't know," Ridley murmured and lunged at Alex, missing when Alex spun out of reach just in time. "Aww, come on." He stalked Alex as Alex backed away with his hands up in defense. "How about a little brotherly love?"

"Eww. Eww." Alex faked a dodge to the right—"Eww"—then jumped to the left instead.

Ridley anticipated the movement and hit Alex in the gut with his shoulder, lifting him off his feet. "Jesus." Alex flailed, trying to grab something, and ended up over Ridley's shoulder looking at his back. "Put me down," he squeaked.

"C'mon, big brother. Teach me about the birds and the bees."

"Okay, that's just sick," Alex complained and slapped Ridley on the ass. "Now put me down." Christ, Ridley was strong. Alex wasn't used to being manhandled. He did the manhandling but—he kneaded Ridley's firm butt cheeks—he kind of liked it.

Ridley stopped, his body stiffening, and he whistled and hummed. "Oh wow," Ridley drawled and set Alex on his feet.

Alex followed Ridley's gaze out the patio window. "Oh wow," he echoed.

"Now a man could get used to a view like that," Ridley commented appreciatively and opened the sliding glass door, allowing Alex to step out on the deck ahead of him.

It wasn't a beach, more like marshland, but a large deck had been constructed from the backyard across the marsh to the open blue water. Tied up at the end of the dock was a small fishing boat. Not only did they have an amazing ocean view, but they also had an amazing outdoor space complete with rattan seating areas, wooden tables, a gas barbeque, and a fricking pool! Mick definitely made up for his little joke with this place.

"Holy shit, we're right on the ocean," Alex said in awe.

"Actually Hackberry isn't on the ocean. That's Calcasieu Lake," Ridley corrected. "But it is amazing, isn't it?"

"How the hell do you know so much about this place?" Alex asked, cutting a sideways glance toward Ridley.

"While you were busy complaining about Agent Daigle's driving skills, I was tuning you out by reading a pamphlet I picked up on West Calcasieu Parish at the gas station."

"I wasn't complaining. I was critiquing them," Alex said wryly.

"Uh-huh," Ridley hummed, sounding skeptical. "Man, I say we check out the rest of this place and then head out and do a little fishing. What ya think?" he asked and draped an arm over Alex's shoulders.

When he'd been dropped into Slater during the middle of the night, Alex hadn't been feeling all warm and fuzzy about it. He'd always had a very active work and social life. He was used to having people around him, so the idea of holing up in a small, sterile white place in the middle of the woods, alone, had totally sucked. It took him weeks before he had pulled his sappy, lonely ass up out of the dumps. As Alex tried to discreetly push a little closer into Ridley's side as they stood there looking out over the ocean—the lake—he knew this time was going to be different. Hell, he'd be happy if he didn't see another person for the next few weeks except Ridley. He wasn't sure what that meant, but he refused to look too deeply at the way Ridley made him feel… well… warm and fuzzy.

"Fishing sounds like a great way to spend the evening," Alex responded with a wide grin. "Let's go check out the digs."

IN CONTRAST to the amazing outside space and views, the inside area of the house was much more humble. Built in the nineteen thirties, it had original hardwood floors throughout, glass-paned french doors between the living and dining room, and all original wood trim and cabinetry. It kind of reminded Ridley of his grandma's home, less the feminine touches, horrid wallpaper, and stench of mothballs.

As they explored their new living quarters, Ridley found himself grinning like a fool, something he'd been doing a lot since they'd left

Slater. It wasn't that he didn't know the danger they were in, but the whole experience was surreal and it felt more like he was an actor in an action film with a really sexy costar as a sidekick. Eventually the well of emotions he felt for what his family and friends would have to endure would overwhelm him with guilt, but there wasn't a damn thing he could do about their pain and to dwell on it wasn't going to make the situation better or change anything. So instead he focused on the excitement and joy he felt getting to spend time with Alex.

"Now this is almost as great as the back deck," Alex murmured as he ran his hand down one of the thick wooden posts on the large king-size four-poster bed in the master bedroom.

Ridley gave him a questioning look. "Dude, I'm sorry, but I don't care how cool this looks," he said, sitting on the mattress and bouncing up and down a couple times, "or how comfortable, it's still not as great as the view from the deck or the pool."

"I wasn't talking about the look or the comfort." Alex smirked and then walked over and opened the closet door. "Tiny," he commented. "Good thing I don't have a lot of clothes and you have none."

"We're going to have to do some shopping soon. Your jeans are a little tight on me," Ridley commented.

"I like 'em tight." Alex opened another door. It was a small en suite.

"I'm talking about the jeans, not my ass," Ridley chuckled and checked out the bathroom over Alex's shoulder. It wasn't anything special. Just a stand-up shower, sink, and commode, but it was clean and the shower was big enough for two. The idea of a naked Alex, wet and soapy and hot, caused Ridley's dick to perk up and press against the front of his already too-tight jeans.

"I'm talking about both," Alex countered.

Ridley couldn't help but give in to the urge to touch Alex. He wrapped his arms around Alex's waist and pulled him close. Ridley rubbed his growing erection against Alex's ass. "Yeah, and what was it about that bed that put that look on your face and had you thinking it was almost as great as the view?"

Alex pushed his ass back and ground it against Ridley's dick, causing it to swell further and pull a moan out of Ridley. "Did you notice the thickness of those posts?" he asked, still rubbing and swaying.

Ridley let his hand slide down Alex's body, and he cupped the impressive bulge. "Yeah, I did," he murmured against the warm skin of Alex's neck. He squeezed Alex's dick to emphasize his meaning.

Alex laid his hand over Ridley's and pushed it even harder against his dick. "How could you not?" Alex snorted. "It's a fucking monster."

"Big fucking battering ram," he agreed, stroking Alex's even more impressive ego, knowing he'd be rewarded for the efforts.

"Still, I was talking about the posts on the bed." Alex spun in Ridley's arms, grabbing his hips and slamming their groins together. "I want to tie your wrists and ankles to them," Alex growled against Ridley's mouth.

He'd never been tied up before, but the idea of being bound and at Alex's mercy caused a thrill to race down Ridley's spine. "That would be hot," he responded huskily, throat dry.

Alex answered by taking Ridley's mouth in a bruising kiss using teeth and tongue, leaving Ridley breathless with his heart racing and his cock throbbing when it ended.

"But first, I do believe you mentioned wanting to fish," Alex said, his tone teasing as he abruptly released Ridley and stepped past him.

Ridley looked down at the straining bulge in his jeans, a wet spot the size of a quarter obvious. "Damn him and his cockiness," he grumbled. He was in the mood for fishing all right, but the worms and rods he wanted to play with didn't have a damn thing to do with slimy swimming creatures.

"Hey, you come back here," he called out and stalked after Alex.

CHAPTER 16

THE SUN was high in the sky without a single cloud anywhere to be seen. A slight salty breeze kept the eighty-degree temps from being too hot. After enduring the long winter of northern Michigan, this was heaven. Ridley sat up from where he'd been lounging and set his fishing pole in the holder. He hadn't had a bite in over half an hour and didn't care. Messing with a fish would have only interrupted the tranquil peace.

"Toss me another beer, please."

Alex turned his head from where he was resting it against the back of the captain's chair and mumbled sleepily, "Don't wanna move. Man, this is the fucking life, eh?"

"It would be if I had another beer. C'mon, the cooler is right at your feet. You don't even have to get up."

"Demanding little shit," Alex grumbled but reached down, grabbed a beer, and tossed it to him.

Ridley caught it easily, replaced his empty one in his koozy with it, and lounged back against the cushions, stretching out his legs. "Now this is the life," he agreed. He popped the top on his can and took a big gulp.

The sound of the water lapping against the boat and the gentle rocking lulled Ridley, and he stared out toward the horizon as he enjoyed his beer. He'd spent a lot of time fishing with his grandpa when he was growing up, but as soon as he hit his teens, fishing was just a good excuse to drink with his buddies and work on his tan. He was sure his new job as a fisherman wouldn't be as enjoyable as this.

"Do you know anything about commercial fishing?" he finally asked, interrupting the silence.

"Not a thing," Alex admitted. "But how hard can it be to catch a fish?"

"We've had our poles in the water for over an hour and haven't had so much as a nibble," he reminded Alex.

"I didn't put any bait on my hook." Alex chuckled and tossed his empty can into the box and grabbed another beer. "I'm just here for the sun and suds."

"Nice. But I have a feeling fishing for a living is a little different than this." Something occurred to Ridley and he sat up and faced Alex. "Do we even need to make a living or is Uncle Sam footing the bill?"

"Uncle Sam is a fucking tightwad," Alex sniffed. "We don't have to worry about the housing and shit, but if we want to eat or enjoy the finer things in life"—he held up his beer—"then we're gonna have to work. You really think I'd work as a library assistant by choice?"

Ridley studied Alex for a moment. Even with everything he now knew about Alex, his initial impression still fit. "What about in high school?" he asked curiously. "Were you a geek before you went to the police academy?"

Alex sat up and shoved his shades up on his head and looked at Ridley with affronted shock. "Did you seriously just ask me that?"

"There is nothing wrong with being a geek. Hell, it's what first attracted me to you."

"Really?"

"Hell yeah. I remember thinking you worked the fuck out of cute." He winked at Alex who was still looking at him with shock. "I still think you do."

"That's it," he grumped and pulled the shades back down over his eyes. "I'm so shaving my head as soon as we get back."

"What?" Ridley said, alarmed. "You can't!"

"The fuck I can't. It's not very manly to be called cute. And just so you know, I was not a geek in high school. I barely passed. And I'm not sure if I ever walked into a library before Slater. I was a jock, thank you very much." He smirked and flexed his bicep.

"Yeah, so is Kyle," Ridley muttered lowly.

"What was that?"

"Impressive gun," Ridley said, tipping up his beer to hide his grin.

"Uh-huh," Alex hummed dubiously.

"No, seriously, it's impressive. So what kind of sports did you play?"

"Are we going to play twenty questions now?"

"I don't really know that much about you. I mean, I now understand why you didn't like to talk about yourself, but I'm having a difficult time coming to terms with the vision in front of me and the guy who runs out into the path of bullets."

"Not really much to tell," Alex said with a shrug. "Before all this craziness, I had a pretty average life. I grew up in a small middle-class town in southern California. My dad's a factory worker, and my mom is the secretary at the high school I attended."

"That had to suck," Ridley laughed.

"Actually it wasn't too bad, she's pretty cool and I wasn't a troublemaker, but my sister hates it."

"You have a sister?"

"Yup. Emma is only seventeen. My mom had a hard time getting pregnant after me. Anyway, Emma is your typical pain-in-the-ass kid sister. She's also a little pampered princess. I'm kind of her hero since I haven't lived at home since she was ten. I got to miss all the drama of the teenage shit and since I'm not there to scare off the little fuckers who come sniffing around wanting to take her out, we get along pretty good."

"You must miss them. Your family?"

Alex pursed his lips, nodding slowly, and then took a long pull from his beer. "Yeah," he responded curtly and tipped up his beer again.

Ridley could tell by the tenseness in Alex's shoulders and the way he looked away that the subject bothered him. Ridley had only had to think about what his disappearance was going to do to his family for a couple of days; he couldn't imagine the guilt and sadness Alex had had to deal with over the last year and a half.

"Did you always want to be a cop?" Ridley asked, changing the subject.

"Yup, ever since I got my first cap gun. Actually, at first I wanted to be a cowboy, but cop came quickly after that. I got a job as a security guard right out of high school while I took some college courses and entered the academy as soon as I was old enough. Planned on working my way up to homicide detective, but…." Alex downed the rest of his beer and tossed the can in with the other empties. "Well, you know how that turned out."

"You'll have plenty of time to work on your goal once all this is over," Ridley reminded him.

"These people have a long memory, Ridley," Alex muttered. He grabbed his fishing pole and started reeling in the line.

When he didn't say anything further, Ridley asked, "Meaning?"

"Nothing. Reel in your line. I'm getting hungry."

The conversation about Alex's past was effectively over. Ridley knew not to push him. When Alex got that closed-off look on his face, Ridley wouldn't be getting anything more. Still, it hadn't been a total waste; he'd learned more about Alex's home life in the last few minutes than he had in all the months since he'd met him.

Ridley gulped down the last of his beer and disposed of the can. Without a word he reeled in his line and set the pole aside. Alex put the boat in gear and headed back to the dock.

"What about you?"

"Excuse me?" Ridley asked as he took the seat up front next to Alex.

"What about you?" Alex repeated as he ran his gaze over Ridley's tattoos. "Geek or jock?"

"Jock," Ridley chuckled. "Basketball."

"I would have taken you for a burnout."

"You assume wrong and we've already established what happens when one assumes."

"Touché. What's the meaning behind your tats?"

Ridley looked down at his colorful arms. "I don't know that they started out with a meaning, more about rebellion, I think," he said, pointing to an evil-looking devil on his forearm. "Then I realized they should mean something. The road leading up to the sunset on my bicep is about my path to something more, happiness perhaps." He shrugged.

"You find your happiness yet?" Alex asked thoughtfully.

"Yes and no. I had a hard time being bullied when I was young. I'm a lot happier now, but this one is a reminder of who I am now," he said pointing to Underdog on his other forearm and laughing. "Bumbling protector. The basketball, Pokémon, and Mad Hatter are just things I like."

"I like them too. Weird combination, but your artist was brilliant the way he made them all work, complement each other," Alex commented. "What about the Chinese symbols?"

"Those are for my family. They are the symbols for love, strength, and home."

"That's cool. Tell me about your family?"

"Dad's an electrical engineer, Mom takes care of him."

"Brothers and sisters?" Alex asked.

"Nope. I'm an only child. My mom, too, had a problem after she had me. They had to take out her baby-making shit. Mom and Dad thought about adopting, but I guess they figured I was enough."

Ridley's chest constricted and he turned away from Alex, watching the waves hit the side of the boat to hide the sadness that rushed up in him. He wasn't making light of what Alex's parents were going through, but he was all his mom and dad had. There was no irritating kid sister. He might like to give off a bad-boy image with the way he looked, but at heart he was a mama's boy and he hated that he was causing her pain.

It took him a moment to get his emotions under control, reminding himself once again that it wouldn't help anyone to dwell on things he couldn't change. Plus, he reasoned that not knowing what happened to him, being able to hold on to hope had to be a hell of a lot better than actually attending his funeral.

"Hey, look!" Alex called out, pulling Ridley from his morose thoughts.

Ridley looked to where Alex was pointing but saw nothing but blue skies and water. He scanned the area and then spotted gray breaking the surface of the water. One dolphin jumped, followed by two more. "Cool!" Ridley exclaimed.

Alex put the boat in neutral, and they sat silently watching the dolphins jumping and twisting. Ridley was mesmerized by their movements and they calmed him. They continued to watch them until they disappeared into the horizon.

"I suddenly no longer have a craving for fish and chips," Alex drawled. "How about a steak on the grill?"

Ridley nodded, still looking out at the water. "Steak sounds like a damn good idea."

A SUBDUED calm seemed to settle over them, the feeling continuing when they arrived back at the house. Alex took a quick shower, dressing in nothing but a pair of gym shorts. The skin on his shoulders and back had a red tint and was uncomfortable enough that the thought of having to wear a shirt wasn't appealing. He wasn't complaining. Having the chance to spend time in the sun, especially with Ridley, was worth any discomfort. It had been a lazy, comfortable day, something Alex hadn't experienced in a long time. Always looking over his shoulder, staying on edge kept him alive, so he knew to enjoy these rare days when he could. What really shocked him about it, though, was how quickly he felt completely at ease with another person outside of his family. The only other person he'd ever felt this at ease with was Mick, and even that had taken time.

He could hear Ridley humming in the shower, and Alex smiled as he pulled a couple steaks from the fridge. He set them on the counter, and as he rummaged through the cabinet for spices, he found himself humming along to the same tune. He seasoned the steaks, set them aside to marinate, and headed out to the deck to fire up the grill.

When he walked back in, Ridley was coming out of the bathroom, toweling his hair. He wore a pair of Alex's blue-and-white Bermuda shorts, a little tight in all the right places. Water droplets ran down the tanned skin of his chest.

"Damn, my clothes look fucking hot on you," he commented with a sly grin.

Ridley looked down at his shorts and then slowly lifted his gaze to meet Alex's. Without a word he turned, presented his ass, and wiggled it. "A little tight, don't you think?"

"Oh yeah," Alex murmured and landed a hard slap against that tight ass.

"Hey!" Ridley protested, laughing as he spun away before Alex could hit him again. Ridley gripped his damp towel in both hands, threatening Alex with it.

"You snap me with that and I'm going to beat your ass," Alex warned, pointing a finger at him.

"Not a deterrent," Ridley snorted and aimed the towel threateningly.

Alex lunged, grabbing the towel with one hand and wrapping the other around Ridley's body, pulling him hard against himself and pinning Ridley's arm between their bodies. "That comes later when I have you tied to the bed," he told him in a seductive tone. Ridley's eyes fluttered closed and he groaned when Alex nipped his chin. "You like that idea, don't you?" Alex murmured as he licked at Ridley's bottom lip.

"As crazy as it sounds, yeah I do," Ridley admitted and opened his mouth, inviting Alex in.

Alex took the invitation and dove in, exploring Ridley's mouth until they were both breathless when it ended. "I'm going to rock your crazy world later," Alex promised.

"Later?" Ridley questioned and chased Alex's lips when he pulled away. "No time like the present, I've always said."

"You're going to need to eat your protein first," Alex suggested and released him.

"I like the way you think," Ridley agreed, dropping the towel and grabbing the waistband on Alex's shorts, trying to pull them down.

Alex slapped his hand away and chuckled. "Fucking horndog, I was talking about steaks."

"Mmm, tube steak, my favorite."

Alex shook his head and once again spun out of Ridley's grasp. "That was so lame. Just for that, you can make the salad."

"I thought it was clever as hell."

"You would," Alex sniffed. He opened the fridge and started handing Ridley the lettuce and all the fixings.

"And what will you be doing while I'm slaving away?" Ridley asked as he started washing the vegetables.

"I'll be over here admiring the buns I'll be sliding my tube steak into later."

"And you called me lame," Ridley huffed and then laughed.

"You are," Alex said teasingly.

Damn, he liked the sound of Ridley's laugh and the way it caused his belly to flutter pleasantly each time he heard it. Alex still wasn't sure how he felt about this whole new sensation he was feeling for Ridley, and he refused to give it a name or look at it too deeply. That didn't stop him from moving up close to the man once again and placing his lips against the warm flesh of Ridley's shoulder, though.

"You have a nice laugh," he complimented.

Ridley tilted his head and looked at Alex over his shoulder. "Thanks," he responded, sounding almost shy.

"You're welcome. Now get busy on my salad. I'm starving," he demanded and patted Ridley's firm little butt. "I'll get the steaks on."

Ridley started to open his mouth, but Alex shot him a warning look as he picked up the pan with the steaks. "Don't even say it."

The laugh Alex was becoming so fond of followed him out to the deck, and he couldn't help but smile.

CHAPTER 17

THEY WERE living in a bubble. A happy, no drama, no worries, just the two of them bubble. He and Alex had spent the last few days sunning and fishing and fucking like bunnies as if they didn't have a care in the world. Of course, it only felt that way—in actuality they had plenty to be concerned by. The threat of death was a hell of a lot to worry about. Ridley often found Alex up at night watching out the windows, and even when Alex seemed to be completely at ease, Ridley had learned to recognize the signs that he wasn't. The muscles in Alex's shoulders rarely ever relaxed, and he was constantly assessing the area around him. Still, Ridley found himself completely comfortable when he was with Alex. He was sure it was mainly due to the fact that he trusted Alex implicitly and knew within the walls of their temporary home, their bubble, he was safe. Was he a fool? Perhaps, but he couldn't help the way he felt nor his ability to block out the world. He was happy.

He almost regretted venturing out, but a man could only go without his own drawers for so long. And even though Alex liked the way Ridley looked in Alex's one-size too small jeans, Ridley liked pants that gave his junk a little room to move. They'd driven through the great big town of Hackberry, which consisted of a bait-and-tackle store, a gas station, a bar, a church, and little else. He wasn't into the rubber wader look, which was about all he could find in the way of clothing, so they drove into Lake Charles. Alex bitched once again about the stench of sulfur, but other than that he seemed to be in a good mood as they headed down the roadway, jamming to twangy country music.

"I think we should stop for lunch and enjoy the Cajun flare," Alex suggested as he turned down the volume on the radio.

"Sounds good to me, but can I suggest we do it after I get some clothes?"

"But I'm hungry," Alex whined.

"You're always hungry. And stop your whining, it just doesn't work for you," Ridley chastised lightly. For someone as lean as Alex, Ridley was shocked by how much the man could eat and how often. "Plus, I don't want to try on clothes with a full belly."

Alex stuck his tongue out at Ridley playfully. "I don't whine," Alex said with an obvious whine to his tone. "But I am hungry. And why in the hell do you have to try clothes on? Just grab some shorts, T-shirts, and undies and we're outta there."

Ridley dug around in the glove box of the old truck for the goodies he'd stashed just for such an occasion. "Here," Ridley said and thrust the candy bar at Alex. "Eat up."

Alex gave Ridley an exasperated look, but he accepted the candy bar, tore the package open, and took a big bite. "You better have another one in there or I'm stopping for lunch first."

Ridley tossed the other candy bar in Alex's lap. "You're so predictable."

"Only when it comes to my eating habits," he responded, chewing happily.

"Uh-huh. And I have to try on jeans to make sure they fit right. This new trend of short waists sucks. They crush my nuts."

"Levi's 501s, baby. You grab ten pairs, a stack of T-shirts, and a couple packages of socks and undies and, bam, done shopping for a year. Fifteen minutes in the store, tops."

Ridley gave him an incredulous look.

"What?" Alex grumped.

"You're so full of shit. Need I remind you of your bow ties, dress shirts, and skinny jeans? All three of which, by the way, are super hot on you," he added and waggled his brows.

"Don't get used to them. The clothes, like the hair, were part of the Alex Firestone persona. I'm Alex Richmond now, commercial fisherman from Hicktown, USA. There will be no bow ties or skinny jeans."

"You're not cutting your hair," Ridley said adamantly.

"Watch me." Alex smirked.

It was the same argument they'd had since arriving in Hackberry. Alex couldn't wait to cut off what he called his crazy mop, and Ridley begged him not to do it. So far, Alex hadn't done it, but only because Ridley had distracted him with well-timed blow jobs or other sexual diversions each time he attempted to pull out the clippers. He was going to have to get creative with his ploys if he was going to keep Alex from cutting the curls.

"There's a strip mall." Ridley pointed out the window, not commenting on Alex's warning.

Alex pulled into a parking spot in front of a clothing store and put the truck in park. "Don't take all day," he grumbled and pulled his cap down low over his eyes.

"You're not going in with me?"

Alex shook his head and pulled the gun from the center console and held it against his stomach, keeping it out of sight with his T-shirt. Ridley's eyes widened in confusion, but Alex wasn't looking at him, already scanning the parking lot intensely. It was like a switch was flipped and the teasing, fun-loving man was replaced by a serious and tense one.

"I won't be long," Ridley promised. He stepped out of the truck and unease skittered along his spine.

Again he was reminded he wasn't on vacation, but on the run from dangerous individuals who were desperate to eradicate a problem— Alex—who could bring down their entire empire. Ridley was now part of that problem and, as such, needed to be eliminated as well.

Ridley hurried his steps and entered the shop, a blast of cool air from the air conditioner blowing across his sweat-dampened face and causing him to shiver. The bell over the door announced his arrival. From behind the counter a young lady looked up and smiled broadly. "Hi, is there something I can help you find today?" she greeted pleasantly.

Ridley scoped out the store, but relaxed a little when he didn't see any other customers. "Hi," he responded, stepping up to the counter. "I'm going to need a whole new wardrobe."

"Lost a bunch of weight, did ya? Good for you," she complimented and smiled impossibly wider. "I'll be happy to help, I'm Chloe."

Ridley started to say no, then realized it was the perfect excuse. "Thanks, Chloe. I'm going to need socks, shorts, underwear, the works."

He glanced out the window to where Alex was waiting in the truck. "And I'm kind of in a hurry."

"No problem. Let's start over here," she said, curling her finger in a "come with me" gesture as she headed to a display of undergarments.

She turned and faced Ridley, running her gaze down his body, sizing him up. "A thirty-three," she said with a curt nod. "Boxers or briefs?"

"Yes."

Chloe tilted her head, a confused look on her face briefly, but then she laughed and grabbed a package from the shelf. "One pack of boxer briefs, black. You don't seem like the tighty-whitey type."

"Good call. Better make it two," he said with a wink.

Chloe, an attractive little redhead in what Ridley guessed was her early twenties, was as flirty as she was helpful. He chuckled at the seductive looks she kept giving him, but only nodded and smiled when she flirted and batted her lashes at him. Thankfully, it took no time at all and she had an entire new wardrobe piled up in Ridley's arms and was leading him to the register.

"So where are you from?" she asked while ringing up his purchases.

"What? You don't think I'm from around these parts?" he asked dubiously.

"Not with that accent," she drawled. "Midwest?"

"Yup, you got me."

"What brings you to Lake Charles?" Chloe inquired cheerfully.

"Umm...." Ridley quickly checked out the window. Alex was still sitting behind the wheel of the truck. "Just needed a change of scenery," he said vaguely.

"I don't know how you Yankees handle the winters up there," she said with a visible shudder. "I'd just die in all that snow and Oh. My. God. No sun in the winter? No thank you."

Chloe babbled on about her dislike of the cold, but Ridley was only half paying attention. He couldn't help but keep looking to Alex, feeling as if he'd already made him wait too long.

Ridley pulled the cash Alex had given him from his wallet, hoping the gesture would make Chloe hurry up. Ridley had tried to refuse it, but Alex had insisted, telling him he'd put it on Uncle Sam's tab. Ridley relented, but only after Alex reminded him he couldn't use his bank or credit cards. He wasn't going to buy a whole lot of clothes with the sixteen dollars he had in his wallet. His need for his own underwear outweighed his dislike of Alex buying them.

"That will be three hundred and twenty-four dollars and sixteen cents."

Ridley counted out the bills plus an extra twenty and handed it to her. "Thanks for all your help, Chloe." He grabbed his bags and turned to head out the door.

"If you need anyone to show you around town, just let me know. I work every day but Tuesday and Friday," she called out to him.

Sorry, not going to happen. "Thanks, I'll keep that in mind," he responded and pushed out the door before she insisted he take her number.

"Took ya long enough," Alex grumbled as soon as Ridley slid into the truck.

"Not my fault the sales clerk had the hots for me and wanted to keep me in there. Sheesh, I thought I was going to get mauled over a rack of jockstraps."

"You should have told her you liked to get fucked rather than do the fucking," Alex remarked crudely as he fired up the truck.

Ridley looked toward the store to see if he could see inside through the large window, but the sun was shining on it, making it impossible for him to see inside. "How do you know it was a she and not a hot guy?"

Alex shot him a smug look without comment before pulling out of the parking space and headed out of the lot.

"Well?" Ridley pressed.

"Her name is Chloe, she talks way too fucking much, hates the cold, and offered to be your guide around town."

Ridley gaped at Alex.

"How'd I do?" he asked smugly.

"How the hell did you know that?" Ridley squeaked. "You couldn't even see inside the window with the way the sun was shining on it."

"Because I'm just that good," he responded with a nonchalant shrug. "Now can we go eat? I'm starving."

Ridley shifted in his seat until he was facing Alex and stared at him incredulously. No way could Alex have seen inside the store, let alone have heard what he and Chloe were talking about. "No we cannot go eat until you tell me how in the hell you did that?"

"I told you I'm just that good," Alex snorted.

"Bullshit! How the hell—" Ridley narrowed his eyes and glared at Alex. "You have me bugged?"

"Now would I do that?" he said with a dismissive wave.

"Yes. Yes you would." Ridley pulled on the neck of his T-shirt and looked down at his chest, then checked his arms, legs, and pockets.

"What the hell are you looking for?"

"Wires," he said, pulling off a shoe and inspecting it—nothing. He pulled off the other one and didn't find anything in that one either. "I don't know how you did it, but you had to have wired me or something."

"You're paranoid," Alex chuckled. "How about Bayou Grill?"

"Bayou Grill?" he asked distractedly, still searching for the wire he knew had to be somewhere on his body. It was the only thing that made sense.

"For lunch."

"Dammit, Alex, where is it?"

"It's right there," Alex said, pointing out the window. "Good thing too. Did I mention I was starving?"

"That's not what I was talking about and you damn well know it," Ridley complained.

Ridley pulled out his wallet, searching every flap and pocket as well as the cards and IDs, but again found nothing.

"Mmm, all-you-can-eat crawfish. Sounds right up my alley," Alex commented happily. "Ready?"

Ridley looked up to see they had come to a stop outside a restaurant. "I'll figure this out," he promised and stepped out of the truck.

"So, how long have you had this problem with paranoia?" Alex asked as he followed Ridley out of the truck. He hit the key fob and then met Ridley at the front, barely able to conceal his grin.

"Bite me."

"Name the place and time, baby," Alex purred and then chomped his teeth together.

Ridley rolled his eyes. "I'll figure it out," he repeated under his breath.

CHAPTER 18

STEPPING INTO Bayou Grill, Ridley was taken aback by the décor. The walls were a bright yellow with drawings of ferryboats painted on them. Colorful Mardi Gras posters hung throughout as well as old musical instruments. Multicolored lights were strung along the ceiling. The floors were a rustic tile, and the tables were covered with brown paper. It was gaudy, but the scents of strong creole spices of garlic, onion, and cayenne pepper were inviting and caused Ridley's gut to growl loudly. He took in the delicious aroma and momentarily put aside his need to find out what the hell Alex had been up to.

"Sit wherever you like," a young man called out as he walked by with a tray of drinks.

Alex led them to a booth in the corner and slid in. From their seats they could view the entire main area of the restaurant, which was occupied by one other couple. Alex picked up the menu that was stuck in the holder in the center of the table and handed it to Ridley and then sat back as he took in the restaurant.

"Interesting-looking place, huh?" Ridley asked as he scanned the menu.

"I just hope the chef is better than their decorator. Did I mention I was starving?"

"Maybe once or a hundred times," Ridley muttered with a shake of his head.

"Just wanted to make sure you knew." Alex smirked.

"Hi, I'm Crosby. Welcome to Bayou Grill. Can I start you with something to drink?" the waiter asked with a broad smile.

He was tall and thin, dressed in jeans and a T-shirt with the restaurant logo on it. Dark hair and eyes as well as his deep tan gave him an exotic look. Crosby was a very attractive man and looked to be about the same age as he and Alex.

"I'll have sweet tea, but I'm also ready to order. I'll have the all-you-can-eat crawfish and a bowl of gumbo, please," Alex ticked off. "And there's an extra tip if you bring it quick."

"Yes, sir, and for you?" Crosby asked, looking to Ridley.

"Crap, I haven't even looked yet," Ridley muttered as he scanned the menu. "Umm, I'll have...."

He wasn't really sure since everything sounded so good. He loved Cajun food, the spicier the better. His mom's sister had lived in New Orleans when she was younger, learning to cook all the authentic dishes of the region. She often made the most amazing spicy dishes when they'd visit her.

Alex cleared his throat and thrummed his fingers against the tabletop.

"Oh sorry," he muttered in apology. "I'll have the chicken andouille gumbo and the shrimp etouffee," he said and returned the menu to its holder.

"Both excellent choices," Crosby praised. "And to drink?"

"Sweet tea is fine."

"Very well. I'll get these in right away and bring your drinks."

"Guess I'm not the only one starving," Alex murmured and tipped his cap back on his head, the movement exposing a small wire near Alex's ear.

That solved the mystery as to how Alex could have known what he and Chloe had been discussing. Ridley wasn't upset. He wouldn't doubt if they were constantly under surveillance of some sort—though hopefully not while in the bedroom since that might be a little uncomfortable and awkward. With the way Alex had tried to act like he was just all that badass, all-knowing, however, he deserved a little payback. Ridley would have to give it some thought.

Crosby dropped their drinks off as well as set a large plate of steaming crawfish in front of a salivating Alex. "Oh God," Alex groaned.

"These look delish. Help yourself," he offered to Ridley as he grabbed one and pulled the head off.

"Nah, I'm good," Ridley declined.

"You don't know what you're missing," Alex countered and sucked on the end of the head before tossing it aside and cracking open the shell. "Oh well, all the more for me."

"That's nasty," Ridley muttered and wrinkled his nose.

"What's nasty?" Alex asked as he chewed, humming a little, and popped another head off a crawfish. Once again he stuck the head into his mouth and sucked it.

"That right there," Ridley pointed out. "Sucking the head."

"I thought you got off on it when I sucked a little head." Alex smirked and made a grand gesture of sucking the crawfish head, adding in slurping noises and low moans.

"The heads I suck don't end in me having a mouthful of fish brains," he said in disgust and took a big gulp of his tea. "Now have some manners, man." He tossed his napkin at Alex. "And clean yourself up. Should I see if Crosby can bring you a bib?"

"Might be a good idea." Alex popped another hunk of meat in his mouth, still moaning in delight.

Ridley did his best to ignore Alex and his less-than-stellar eating habits, knowing if he kept commenting it would only egg the bastard on. Alex wasn't making it easy. The little porn noises he was making caused images of the man on his knees sucking on a different kind of treat to pop into Ridley's head. His dick twitched in response. Yet another thing he was so going to pay Alex back for.

Ridley was achingly hard and gritting his teeth by the time Crosby brought the rest of their food. The smug look on Alex's face was evidence he knew exactly what he was doing to Ridley.

"I'll be right back," Ridley grumbled and slipped out of the booth.

"Where ya going? Your food's gonna get cold."

Ridley didn't comment, discreetly trying to adjust his overly tight jeans as he made his way to the bathroom. He should have known Alex would pull something like this and worn a pair of his new, looser-fitting jeans out of the shop. Fucker got off on seeing him squirm.

ALEX HELD his laughter in by biting down on his lip as Ridley walked stiffly to the bathroom. Damn sexy fucker was so much fun to tease. It didn't take much to get him riled up, which was awesome for their sex life. Ridley got hard when the wind blew. But he also had a quick wit, which meant there was a lot of laughter as well.

Fun didn't mean Alex had lowered his guard, but he hadn't seen anything that had caused alarm bells to go off and he let himself relax a little as he continued to eat. Alex picked up his tea to take a sip, his arm stopping midmotion when he heard a low moan.

He glanced around himself but was unable to find the source of the noise. The other couple was chattering happily across the room, and Crosby was nowhere in sight. Shrugging it off, Alex took a large gulp of his tea.

"God, so hard."

Alex jerked his head from right to left. He was sure he'd heard someone, but with their table against the back wall there was no one behind him. Perhaps the walls were paper thin, he mused.

"Mmm, feels so good." The disembodied voice was followed by a rhythmic slap that sounded suspiciously like someone jerking off.

"What the hell?" Alex muttered and checked under the table. Of course no one was there but he was running out of places to look. It made no sense.

"Oh yeah, Alex, suck my cock."

Alex's brows raised and he tilted his head, straining to listen as he realized it was Ridley's voice he was hearing. He reached up and untucked the wire earphone from his cap and pushed it into his ear.

"Uh.... Ah.... Love it when you fuck my ass with your finger. Oh yeah, shove it deeper."

Alex's cock instantly hardened at the naughty images Ridley was painting and the deep seductive tone of his voice. Alex pressed his palm against the bulge in his jeans and shifted in the booth.

"Oh yeah, baby. Shove another one in me. Harder. Faster." The rhythm of the slaps of palm to dick sped up.

Alex gritted his teeth and closed his eyes. He was so going to spank that naughty ass as soon as Ridley got back to the table.

"I'm going to come so hard. Fill that sexy mouth of yours so full. Mmm. Oh yeah, Alex…. Oh yeah…. Use those teeth."

"Is there anything wrong with your dinner?"

Alex's eyes flew open to find Crosby standing across the table from him with a concerned expression.

"Play with my balls. Squeeze 'em hard."

"I'm…." *Slap Slap Slap.* Alex squeaked and he cleared his throat. "Everything is fine, thank you," Alex said with a tight smile.

"Feel how hard you make me? Do you like it? Like the way my cock is pulsing?"

Slap Slap Slap.

Alex groaned.

"Are you sure?" Crosby inquired further. "You don't look so good, sir."

Spanking was too light a punishment for the naughty man. He was going to beat that ass. *Slap Slap Slap. "Fuck me harder with those fat fingers"* Ugh. Right after he fucked it, that was, then he'd beat it or bite it or…. Alex squeezed his eyes shut as his dick began to throb painfully with each beat of his racing heart.

"Sir?"

"I'm fine," Alex gritted out, forcing his eyes open.

"Oh God, I'm gonna blow. You ready for my load?"

"Could I get another glass of tea, please?"

"Yes, sir. Right away."

"Oh…. Oh…." The steady slapping sound lost its rhythm, becoming erratic as Ridley's panting breaths came through the earphone.

Alex groaned again, his cock bent at an awkward position within the confines of the tight denim fabric of his jeans. He shifted in his seat, trying unsuccessfully to relieve the pressure, as his ears were filled with the sounds of Ridley moaning and cursing and babbling incoherent nonsense. Sweat dampened Alex's brow and trickled down his temples.

"Yeah. Yeah. Yeah. Oh fuck, here it comes."

Crosby set a fresh glass of tea on the table, his eyes wide as he stared at Alex. "Do you need me to call an ambulance?"

"I'm coming." Slap Slap Slap. "Take it all baby. Swallow that big load. Ah!"

Alex leaned forward and banged his head on the table, waving a dismissive hand at Crosby. "No need for a doctor," he assured the waiter and pounded his hand down on the table to keep from coming in his jeans. "Hot, just really fucking hot. Bread, please," he groaned.

Crosby chuckled and thankfully scurried off.

Alex had barely gotten himself under control when he spotted Ridley coming out of the bathroom with a big satisfied grin on his face. The bastard literally sauntered to the table and slid into the booth.

"What the hell was all that about?"

Ridley picked up his fork, stabbed it into a shrimp, and popped it in his mouth. "I think I drank too much coffee this morning. Man, was I full. I just kept going and going," Ridley said as he chewed. "Wow, this is really spicy, isn't it? No wonder you're sweating." He grabbed his tea and took a sip, but it wasn't enough to hide his grin.

"You do realize this means war," Alex hissed.

"I'm sure I have no idea what you're going on about. Man, you're literally shaking from the heat. Mind if I try some?" Ridley asked, pointing at Alex's gumbo with his fork.

Alex pulled the bowl out of his reach and glared at the irritating little shit. Ridley shrugged and stabbed another shrimp from his own plate.

Crosby showed up with a basket of assorted breads and a glass of milk and set them down in front of Alex. "Sometimes a little milk helps with the heat."

Ridley covered his mouth with his hand, his cheeks turning red, and he began to shake.

"Thank you, that'll be all," Alex informed the waiter.

Crosby looked at Ridley with a questioning look but didn't comment. The minute he walked away, Ridley burst out laughing. "I usually use the milking technique when I'm hot too," he gritted out around snorts of laughter.

"Just you wait," Alex growled.

He grabbed a bread stick and munched on it while Ridley continued to laugh boisterously. Ridley ignored the glares Alex was shooting at him, but eventually the giggles slowed and he wiped away the tears that had rolled down his face and took a big gulp of his tea.

Ridley tapped a finger against his chin and took on a thoughtful expression. "If I didn't know any better, I would swear you had me bugged." He cocked his head and studied Alex for a moment and then waved a hand. "Oh, silly me, there goes my paranoia again."

Alex didn't comment, instead continuing to chomp on his bread. He knew when he'd been outplayed and it was best to keep his mouth shut, at least for now. He may have lost this battle, but he most certainly hadn't lost the war.

CHAPTER 19

AN UNFAMILIAR rusted Chevy truck sat in the drive. Alex, instantly on high alert, reached for his gun when he spotted an older man sitting on the front porch of their home.

"Who is that?" Ridley asked in alarm.

"I don't know." Alex steered the truck slowly down the driveway with his knee as he pulled his service revolver from its holster, checked the clip, and shoved it home. "Get your head down," he ordered Ridley.

Alex leaned over slightly toward the door. The sun was shining directly onto the front windshield, which made it difficult for him to see, but that would make it impossible for the stranger to see within the truck. He pulled to a stop and studied the man on the porch without cutting the engine.

The stranger was dressed in a denim snap shirt and jeans and had a baseball cap pulled low over his eyes. His white hair curling out from beneath the cap matched the color of his short, trimmed beard. As Alex continued to watch him, the man seemed completely relaxed as he spit a dark stream of chew that landed on the sand next to the walkway.

Alex pulled his extra revolver from the console and handed it to Ridley. "Keep your head down and stay in the truck," he demanded. He pushed open the door but didn't step out, gun at the ready. "Can I help you?" he hollered.

"I don't rightly think so, since I'm here to help you," the stranger responded and spit again.

"Excuse me?" Alex asked in confusion. "You're here to help me?"

"That's what I just said, ain't it?" The older man looked down at his watch and tapped it. "Mick said you'd probably be late. Time's a-wastin', boy."

"Mick sent you?" Alex asked suspiciously. "He didn't tell me you were coming."

"He said you'd say that too. Now put that damn gun away and get your ass out here if you want to learn about fishin' and baitin'."

Typical Ramirez. Bastard probably giggled his fool head off when he set this little lesson up. Alex hated not knowing what the hell was going on, a trait Mick knew. He needed to get himself one of those little flip notebooks Mick always had to keep notes. Alex's would be full of all the shit he owed his partner for.

"Keep the gun concealed under your packages when you get out and keep your eyes and ears open. Got it?" Alex slid his gaze toward Ridley long enough to see him nod his understanding, then holstered his gun and stepped out of the truck.

"You have me at a disadvantage. Apparently you know me, but I haven't a clue as to who you are."

The man pushed up from the porch and met him halfway, shaking the hand Alex held out. "Ron Porter. Friends call me Cap." He took a step back, wiping his hand on his jeans, and spit off to the side. "I've known Mick since he was knee-high to a grasshopper. He's told me all about you. You can call me Ron," he drawled, but his green eyes had a mischievous twinkle in them.

"Don't believe everything he tells you. Mick's been hit on the head one too many times. This is Ridley," Alex told him, stabbing a thumb over his shoulder.

Ron cocked his head, brows furrowed as he watched Ridley join them. "Funny, you two don't look nothing like brothers," he pointed out.

"That's 'cause he was adopted," Ridley said. "They took away his mama's parental rights after she dropped him on his head one too many times. It's why he and Mick get along so well."

Alex elbowed Ridley in the ribs, causing him to yelp.

"I like you. *You* can call me Cap," Ron said to Ridley. "Now put that gun away before you shoot yourself and follow me. I don't have a lot of time here."

Alex and Ridley shared stunned glances and did as they were told. From the back of his truck, Ron pulled out a wire box with a rope and a bright yellow buoy with a large dot tied to it and set it on the ground. Ron then pulled a folded piece of paper from his shirt pocket and handed it to Alex. "That there is a map of where my crab traps are. I've marked the ones you'll be tending to."

Alex unfolded the map: small red Xs marked numerous spots on the lake. "Blue crabs? I thought we were gonna be commercial fishing."

Ron stared at Alex unblinking for a moment and then shook his head. "Trap sits on the bottom of the lake just like that. This here buoy is my distinctive color. You'll pull the boat up alongside one, hook it, and pull the trap to the surface."

He flipped the trap over and released a hook connected to a thick rubber band. "Bait fish goes in here. Make sure it's good and full, then rehook it." Ron flipped the trap back over. "Make sure you don't get your rope tangled up and then drop it in just like this." He let go of the trap—it landed with the bait door against the gravel. "Then move on to the next one. As long as the weather holds you should be able to pull two hundred a day."

"How do you get the crabs out?" Ridley asked, studying the trap.

"Crabs crawl in through those little openings on the sides. Once they get in they can't get back out. You unhook that there top hook, pull it open a bit, turn it over, and shake 'em out into a crate."

"Looks easy enough," Alex commented.

"Let me know if he still feels that way after he's pulled all two hundred," Ron told Ridley with a smirk and threw the trap back into his truck. "I left plenty of crates and burlap sacks down on the dock. Make sure you keep the sacks wet and lay them over the crabs during the day. It keeps them from drying out and crawling out of the crate."

"Thanks, we really appreciate you taking the time to show us how these work. I'm going to go drop these bags off in the house. Can I get you something to drink?" Ridley offered.

"Well, Missus is expecting me home. She's got some projects for me to tend to," Ron drawled and wiped a hand across his brow. "But a man's gotta stay well hydrated in this heat. I'll take a beer if ya got one."

"One ice-cold beer coming up." Ridley met Alex's gaze. "How about you, can I get you something? It won't take me no time at all to whip up one of my famous milkshakes you like so much."

You just keep right on adding on those swats. "I think I'll save that for later," Alex said with a wink. "Beer is fine."

As soon as Ridley was out of earshot, Alex turned to Ron. "So what exactly has Mick told you about me?"

"That you're arrogant, hot-headed, and constantly breaking the rules."

"Pretty much sums me up," Alex agreed. "But usually he adds foul-mouthed to the list."

"Yeah, he mentioned that too." Ron pulled a handkerchief from his pocket and swiped it across his brow as he leaned against the side of his truck. "You've also managed to make some very powerful enemies."

Alex tensed. "We all manage to make a few in our lives," he demurred.

"Not quite like this," Ron said with complete seriousness. "I spent my entire career trying to take them down and you do it by just taking a piss. Don't seem quite right, does it?"

"You're a Fed?"

"Retired."

Alex ran a hand over his jaw. "Now I see why Mick picked this place. He figured I needed a babysitter, did he?"

"The piss-poor pension I get isn't worth getting my ass shot at for a hot head," Ron snorted. "But I want nothing more than to see that piece of shit Gutierrez rotting behind bars, so you can bet your sweet ass I'll be keeping an eye on you. On the back of that map you'll find some random numbers. Read them counterclockwise from bottom center around. It's coordinates that have nothing to do with crab trap placement. You even suspect you've been compromised, you and Ridley get your asses there double time. Understand?"

The screen door banging shut caused them both to look toward the house to see Ridley coming down the stairs with three beers. "Got it. I feel like James Bond with all this secret codes shit. Do I get some really cool spy gadgets? Should I eat the map once I memorize the coordinates?"

Ron reached in the back of his truck and pulled out a long wooden handle with a large metal hook on the end. "Here ya go, but I wouldn't suggest eating that map unless you want to find yourself floating around the gulf, lost."

Alex studied the tool in his hand. "Bond had way cooler gadgets," he grumped. "I'm gonna file a complaint with the higher-ups."

Ron met Alex's gaze, his expression serious. "You just make sure you keep yourself alive long enough to do exactly that, you hear me?"

Ron didn't have to worry. Come hell or high water, Alex was going to live plenty long enough to file that complaint. He had Ridley to protect. Failure was not an option. Alex gave a curt nod just as Ridley stepped up and handed them their beers.

"SO WHAT were you and Ron talking about earlier?"

Alex grabbed Ridley's hand and pulled him down on the lounge chair. He shifted to make enough room so Ridley was lying on his side next to Alex. "He was telling me how he thought I would make a perfect captain and you my trusty first mate."

"Yeah I'm sure that's what it was," Ridley sniffed. He propped his head up on his hand and looked down at Alex. "Seriously. You don't have to tell me exactly what he said. Just tell me should I be worried or need to sleep with a gun under my pillow and one eye open?"

"I'm not going to lie to you, Ridley. You are in danger and I don't want you to take that lightly for a moment. But the arrival of Ron neither increased nor diminished those risks, okay?"

"Okay," Ridley said with a nod. He shifted again until they were both able to look out over the lake.

The sun would be setting soon and lying out on the lounger to watch it drop below the horizon had quickly become their evening ritual. It was fast becoming one of Alex's favorite parts of the day now that he was comfortable enough to get Ridley to snuggle with him. The only thing that might give it a run for its money at the top was waking up each morning wrapped in Ridley's arms.

He was definitely beginning to see the appeal of relationships versus hookups. Not that that was what he and Ridley had—he pressed a kiss to Ridley's temple. Yup, definitely appealing.

"What was that for?" Ridley asked, giving Alex a quizzical look.

"'Cause I can."

"Well, I kind of liked it," Ridley chuckled. He took Alex's hand in his and entwined their fingers.

Alex looked down at their hands. The warmth spreading through him stunned him for a moment until he realized he'd never held hands with a lover before. Hell, the only other men he'd held hands with were his daddy and grandpa when he was a boy. Oh dear God, he was turning in to a total sap, love songs playing in his head and butterflies fluttering around in his belly simply from Ridley's hand in his.

Alex pulled his hand free and shifted out of the chair. "I'm going to grab a beer before the show. You want one?"

"Sure," Ridley responded, seemingly unaware of the discomfort he'd just caused Alex. He stretched his arms up over his head and crossed his ankles, looking totally at ease as he stared out toward the water.

Alex's hands were shaking as he pulled two bottles from the fridge. He leaned back against the counter, chuckling at himself. Jesus, if Mick saw him, he'd never live this shit down. He could hear it now, a badass motherfucker brought to his knees from holding hands. Insanity.

He was totally comfortable with the role of protective cop, and he was obviously way comfortable with the role of fuck buddy and really good at it. He was also quickly discovering that he and Ridley had a lot in common, made each other laugh, and even if they hadn't been forced together by circumstance, they would have become good friends. But this? Whatever this was he was feeling was totally new and left him a little off balance. He hated being off balance.

"All right, Castren, get it together. It was a little hand-holding, not a marriage proposal," he mumbled under his breath. "You got this shit."

Feeling a little better after his pep talk, Alex pushed away from the counter and rejoined Ridley.

"Here ya go," he said, handing Ridley one of the beers and nudging him over as he took a seat next to him. "To another beautiful sunset." He held up his beer.

"Cheers," Ridley said, clinked his bottle against Alex's, and took a long pull.

They sat silently watching the sun as it began its decent below the horizon, putting on a mesmerizing show as rays of red, yellow, and orange sparkled along the rolling waves.

The magical sights, the cooler breeze blowing, and the sounds of gulls crying stripped away the last of the unease Alex felt. He slid his free hand into Ridley's, entwining their fingers again, and tipped his beer up, gulping down half. No love songs started playing in his head, although the butterflies were still a little flighty. It was nice.

They sat there hand in hand, neither saying a word, long after the sun went down and they'd finished their beers. It was Ridley who first broke the tranquility. He pulled his hand from Alex's and went to his feet, arched his back as he stretched, and then scratched his belly. The way Ridley moved, seeing all the smooth, tanned skin, was as captivating as the sunset had been. *Mmm.* A tune was back in Alex's head, but this time instead of a sappy love song, it was more in line with a little Barry White and "Let's Get It On." *That* feeling he totally understood.

Ridley caught Alex staring at him, and he raised his brows and smiled. He pressed out his chest and sauntered toward the patio door, putting a little extra sway in his walk.

"How about you come on back here and sway on me," Alex suggested.

Ridley opened the sliding glass door and stopped with his hand on the handle and met Alex's gaze. "Maybe later. I was going to go make a milkshake."

"You little shit!" Alex hooted, being reminded of the shenanigans Ridley pulled at the restaurant. Alex bolted out of the lounger and chased after a laughing Ridley. "Let the ass beatings commence."

CHAPTER 20

IT DIDN'T take long for Ridley to realize blue crabbing was nothing like fishing with a rod and reel. It was a lesson he'd learned on the very first day. Alex had learned it the next day. After not even a week, his and Alex's morning conversation over coffee was completely consumed by arguing over who was going to be captain that day.

This morning Ridley had lost the fight. Damn Alex and his dimples and long lashes anyway. He'd better learn to step up his game and figure out how to become immune to Alex's cuteness or he was going to end up being the one on the wrong end of these goddamn buoys on a daily basis. Problem was, Alex had been working the fuck out of cute since he'd first met him, and the bastard knew how to play Ridley like a puppet.

Ridley blew out a heavy sigh as he hooked the bright yellow buoy. It was definitely going to be a long crabbing season.

He pulled the rope, bringing the blue crab trap to the surface, grumbling and cursing under his breath. The stinky salt water stung the open wounds on his hands and arms. This was why he'd done well in high school, kept his grades up, and worked his ass off to get a scholarship to Slater University. Being a common laborer, even with a half-naked coworker to ogle all day, was so not worth it.

Gripping the wire trap, Ridley shook the crabs into the crate and fastened it back up before turning it over and popping open the bait well. He wrinkled his nose in disgust as he grabbed a handful of half-rotten fish and shoved them into the trap. Careful not to allow the buoy to get tangled up, he threw it back into the water.

"How the hell did I get stuck pulling traps again today?" Ridley grumbled and wiped his slimy hands on his apron.

"Because I have a boo-boo," Alex reminded him, holding up his bandaged finger.

Ridley grabbed the edge of the boat as Alex put it in gear and took off to the next trap. "You have a little cut," he yelled over the roar of the outboard engine.

Alex threw the throttle in neutral next to the next buoy, pitching Ridley forward, and his feet slipped on the wet deck. He flailed momentarily but caught himself at the last minute. Alex ignored the sneer Ridley threw his way, a broad smile on his face. "Besides, I'm captain of this ship and you, my trusty first mate, will do as I say."

"Is that so?" Ridley asked challengingly and snagged the buoy, repeating the process—open, shake, stuff, toss it back—when it hit him and he narrowed his eyes. "Captain, huh?"

"Yup, and as captain I have control of my ship. Now back to work, matey," Alex demanded with a really bad impression of a pirate and hit the throttle.

After the initial thrust forward leveled off, Ridley threw his gloves to the deck and pulled off his apron, tossing it aside as he stalked toward Alex. By the time Alex pulled up to the next buoy, Ridley was standing behind Alex's chair, staring down at him.

"Hey," Alex squeaked when he turned to find Ridley unexpectedly standing so close.

"Control of your ship huh?" Ridley asked dubiously, raising one brow as he spoke.

"Total control," Alex responded with a sly grin.

I'll show you control, Ridley mused silently. He was so going to wipe that cocky look off Alex's face. Clutching the back of Alex's chair, he spun him around and placed his hands on the armrests. Ridley leaned in close until their noses were practically touching. "Care to put a little wager on your abilities to captain your vessel?" Ridley drawled.

Alex stared at him suspiciously for a few heartbeats, his expression thoughtful. "Sure," he finally responded.

"If you can stay in complete control of your *vessel*," Ridley offered, hiding his trickery behind a neutral expression and the laughter in his eyes behind his dark shades, "I'll deem you captain and won't bitch about pulling the rest of the traps."

"And if I don't?"

"You pull the rest and I'll captain without gloating. Deal?"

Alex didn't answer right away, simply blinked, no doubt weighing his odds.

Having learned how highly competitive his lover was, Ridley added with a shrug, "Well, if you don't think you can beat me."

"You're on."

Ridley had to press his lips against Alex's to hide his smile, sealing the deal with a kiss.

The man had been wise to be hesitant. One should never make a bet without knowing all the facts. Alex had good instincts and usually always went with his gut, but Ridley was more than slightly pleased that he hadn't this time. In fact he was downright gleeful, not to mention a whole lot smug as he dropped to his knees.

"What the hell are you doing?" Alex stammered as Ridley tugged at the tie on Alex's shorts and pulled the waistband down, exposing his cock.

"Why, checking out your vessel, my captain." Ridley smirked.

"Hey," Alex started to protest, but it turned into a gasp when Ridley slid his fingers beneath Alex's balls and tugged gently. The gasp turned into a moan when Ridley bent farther and swiped his tongue across the flared head of Alex's cock.

"What was that?" Ridley asked as he looked up at Alex from beneath his lashes and then licked his lips.

Alex's gaze settled on the movement of Ridley's mouth, and Ridley licked his lips again, running his tongue around them and then scraping his teeth across the bottom one. Ridley grinned silently to himself as Alex swallowed hard.

"You're cheating," Alex groaned.

"Mmm, look, your vessel is beginning to rev its engines," Ridley said wryly and slid his finger along Alex's hardening shaft. He quickly followed it with his tongue.

"I'm the captain," Alex muttered as if he were trying to convince himself rather than Ridley.

Alex shifted in his seat, the muscles in his legs tightening, resisting. Ridley's grin grew along with his confidence, and he lapped gently from tip to base, dipping in to flick the delicate sac.

Ridley took his time, exploring every bump and ridge. He swirled the tip of his tongue around the sensitive head, dipping into the small slit, until Alex was fully erect and Ridley could feel the pulse throbbing along the thickness. Ridley mouthed Alex's cock, gently scraping his teeth against the delicate flesh, and felt a shudder roll through Alex's body. A droplet of precum oozed from the slit and Ridley lapped at it, the bitter flavor intoxicating.

"I think your vessel just sprang a leak," Ridley teased and took the head into his mouth, sucking hard, working it with tongue and teeth.

"No. No. No." Alex shook his head and sat back, trying to force Ridley to release him.

Ridley followed his movements, taking Alex down farther, humming.

"This is mutiny," Alex groaned. "I won't stand for it." Alex's words had little meaning as his hand landed on the back of Ridley's head and, instead of trying to force him away, pushed him down farther on his cock.

Ridley gagged a little as Alex's cock hit the back of this throat, but he recovered quickly, changing the angle and bobbing his head in a quick rhythm. As he worked Alex's dick with his mouth, Ridley ran a hand from Alex's abdomen to his chest, the slight sheen of sweat slicking the way.

Alex hissed and moaned when Ridley found one of Alex's erect nipples and pinched it between his finger and thumb, rolling it.

"A short, pleasurable cruise, just a.... Oh fuck, that feels good," Alex gasped when Ridley slid a finger back beneath Alex's balls and pressed against his hole.

The waistband of Alex's shorts constricted Ridley's movements and he sat back, letting Alex's cock slip from his lips, red and bobbing, as he grabbed Alex's shorts and shoved them down his legs and off. "That's better," he purred and tossed the shorts behind him.

Alex clutched the arms of his chair and spread his legs, his chest rising and falling rapidly as he panted.

Ridley's own hard cock began to pulse as he took in Alex's flushed skin and the way the sun glistened off the sweat-dampened ridges of his tanned belly. The way Alex's straining cock curved upward made Ridley's mouth water. Damn, he was one sexy son of a bitch, and Ridley couldn't wait to devour him.

Ridley leaned back in, but Alex stopped his movement by placing his palm against Ridley's forehead. "Wait a minute."

"What's the matter, captain?" he inquired, his voice dripping honey as he tilted his head slightly to look up at Alex. "You ready to turn over the wheel?"

Alex growled lowly and slid his hand to the back of Ridley's head and shoved it down. "Why don't you use your smart mouth for something useful?"

Ridley snorted—his lover was so easy to rile up—and gobbled down Alex's cock. As he sucked and licked and bobbed, Ridley reached up and pushed a finger past Alex's lips. Alex moaned and sucked on the digit, imitating Ridley's movements on his cock. Once Ridley's fingers were wet and sloppy, he pulled them from Alex's mouth, causing him to whimper in protest.

Alex's didn't complain long, rather he was grunting and bearing down as Ridley pushed the tip of his wet finger against Alex's opening. The tight ring of muscle resisted the invasion, but a little more pressure and Ridley breached him.

"Ah yeah, deeper," Alex demanded as he thrust his dick up into Ridley's mouth and then pressed down hard, groaning loudly as the movement took Ridley's finger in to the hilt.

That's it, Captain, take control, Ridley silently encouraged. Alex never bottomed but he loved a little ass play with his blow jobs. The combination never failed to get him off quickly.

Holding Ridley's head in both of his hands, Alex rocked back and forth between the two pleasures. The porno sounds Alex was making caused Ridley's cock to twitch hard.

"Oh.... Oh fuck.... No!" Ridley felt Alex stiffen just as he pushed deep into Ridley's throat, realizing his mistake. "I can't.... Oh fucking hell, don't you dare move," he growled.

Got ya, Captain. Ridley swallowed, his throat constricting around the head of Alex's cock.

"Motherfucker!" Alex howled as his back arched and he erupted into Ridley's throat.

Ridley quickly shoved his free hand down the waistband of his shorts and stroked his throbbing cock as he greedily swallowed down every drop Alex pumped down his throat.

Alex slumped back in his chair, babbling what sounded like curses between panting breaths.

Ridley surged to his feet, Alex hissing as Ridley's finger was pulled from his ass. Continuing to stroke himself hard, Ridley shoved down his shorts with his other hand. "This is how a captain drives his vessel," he jeered. One, two more pulls, his toes curled and he shot his load across Alex's softening cock and heaving chest. Once he was spent, Ridley fell forward, landing heavily on Alex, smearing come and sweat between them.

"Asshole," Alex grumbled but Ridley heard the hint of amusement in his voice.

"That's Captain Asshole to you, matey," he snorted and nuzzled the side of Alex's neck, licking the salty flavor from his skin.

Alex grunted and then landed a hard slap to Ridley's ass.

"Ow!" Ridley yelped and jumped up. "You do that again and you'll be walking the plank," he threatened and rubbed his abused cheek.

Alex pulled up his shorts and pulled the towel he'd been sitting on out from under him. He swiped it across the mess on his torso and then threw it to Ridley, who caught it easily. "When we get back to the house, you'll be bouncing on my plank," he sneered.

"Yeah, yeah, yeah," Ridley chuckled. "Now get your ass up. Those traps aren't going to pull themselves, ya know."

Alex continued to grumble but he got up and stomped to the side of the boat. "And just so you know, Captain," Alex called out, his voice dripping with sarcasm. "I didn't agree to do this without bitching."

Ridley plopped his ass in the chair and spun it around. He shoved the throttle forward. "Bitch away, matey," he called back and then flipped the radio on and turned the volume all the way up.

The sun was high in a beautiful clear blue sky. There was a warm salty breeze blowing, cooling his heated flesh, and he had a satisfied cock.

He was in control of the vessel and had the promise of a little plank time later. It was turning out to be an almost perfect day.

He grabbed a soda out of the cooler and then spun the boat around, moving it up close to the buoy they'd drifted away from. Ridley popped the top on the bottle and gulped down the ice-cold liquid as he watched Alex grab the rope and start pulling the trap to the surface, the muscles of his back and arms flexing and bulging as he worked. Alex's mouth moved the entire time, but Ridley couldn't hear him over the radio.

"Now it is perfect."

CHAPTER 21

THE SUN shining down on Ridley's bare back, the warm wind, and the sound of the waves hitting the shore should have had a calming effect on him. He was anything but. Staring down at Alex laid out on a weight bench in nothing more than a pair of shorts as he bench-pressed a bar of heavy weights caused Ridley's pulse to race. He stared, transfixed at Alex's bulging arms and taut chest, each movement of the bar going down and pushing back up like the sway of a hypnotist's pendulum.

How quickly things had changed. Ridley had first been drawn to Alex by his gentle look, his blond hair, and big dimples that gave him almost an angelic look. Not that any of the fantasies he'd had about Alex were angel-like—definitely more devilish. However, even with the naughty thoughts he'd had about the meek library assistant, Ridley had a strong need to protect Alex as well. He found it ironic that Alex was now the one protecting him. While Ridley still had a strong urge to protect and would always have Alex's back, they were now closer to being equals, almost like partners. It was a position Ridley found very appealing. What he wasn't so sure he was comfortable with, though, was how quickly he was falling for Alex.

Alex had jumped from potential fuck buddy to…. *Christ!* He wasn't even sure how to describe what Alex meant to him now. The only thing he knew for certain was that he enjoyed waking up next to Alex every morning, spending their days together, and ending them wrapped in each other's arms. As he stared down at Alex while he continued to work the weights, powerful body straining and handsome face fierce in concentration, Ridley couldn't imagine a day spent without Alex as part of it.

"Ridley?"

"Hmm?" Ridley responded, pulled from his musings.

"Uh... a little help here," Alex grunted. His face bright red, arms shaking as he strained to push the weights up.

"Oh shit, sorry." He grabbed the bar and helped Alex set it in the cradle.

"Whew!" Alex sat up and shook his arms out. "Some spotter you are," he grumbled.

"I got distracted."

Alex looked around and then back at Ridley with a confused expression. "By what?"

Ridley ran his gaze down Alex's sweat-damp body and then back up and raised a brow.

Alex shook his head and grabbed a towel and ran it over his chest and stomach. "I nearly popped a hernia because you were being pervy? That's low, man."

"I would have thought you'd be used to my pervy ways by now," Ridley teased and shoved at Alex. "Now move it, my turn."

"Pushy bastard," Alex huffed. He got off the bench, ran the towel over the vinyl, and then threw it at Ridley.

Ridley didn't even bother trying to catch it, instead he pulled out the towel he had tucked in the waistband of his shorts and laid it on the bench before lying down. He wrapped his hands around the bar, adjusting his grip, and shifted on the bench, feet planted firmly on the ground.

Alex moved to stand near Ridley's head and placed his hands over Ridley's. "I hope I don't get distracted," he commented with a wink.

Ridley stared at him and narrowed his eyes. Alex was apparently trying for innocence, but the glint of mischief shining in his eyes was obvious and ruined the effect. "Just try to keep up," Ridley instructed and shoved up on the bar. Alex chuckled but turned serious quickly and kept his hands hovering over the bar as Ridley did his reps.

They continued to spot each other through their workout, neither of them losing focus as the weights got heavier, the reps harder. By the time Ridley finished his last set, he was soaked in sweat, muscles fatigued and shaking, spent. He lay on the bench as he worked to slow his huffing breath down and wiped the sweat from his burning eyes.

"Good workout," Alex complimented. "I think we should head up to the house. I'm starving."

"When are you not starving?"

"Hey, I worked hard," Alex grumbled. "I deserve food."

While Alex ran each morning and regularly worked out with free weights, the amount of food he could put away on a daily basis was still staggering. Ridley sat up and tossed the towel aside. "I tell you what, come swimming with me and I'll make lunch." He wiped his hand down his sweaty torso and wrinkled his nose. "I need to get the stink off."

"Last one there does dishes," Alex challenged as he broke out into a run.

"You're such a damn cheat," Ridley called out and chased after the laughing bastard.

The minute Ridley hit the cool water, he couldn't care less about competing or dishes or anything else other than how glorious it felt on his heated flesh. Alex, on the other hand, was in full competitive mode. When Ridley broke the surface, Alex pounced, grabbing Ridley in a bear hug from behind and shoving him back under the water. They spun and rolled, hands sliding on wet skin. Ridley kicked, grabbed, and twisted until he had Alex in a headlock. Ridley made one critical mistake: he underestimated Alex. As Ridley laughed in triumph, Alex pushed back, spun, and Ridley sucked in a large amount of water rather than air.

Ridley popped up and started coughing hard, his eyes bulging as he struggled to get the water out of his lungs. When he couldn't catch his breath, he began to panic. Thankfully Alex didn't. He spun Ridley, pressing a fist beneath Ridley's diaphragm, and gave a couple sharp thrusts, helping to expel the water and allowing Ridley to breathe again.

"That's enough excitement for one day," Alex commented and released his hold on Ridley. "Besides, I'm—"

"Hungry," Ridley finished for him. "I nearly die and you're worried about your stomach."

"A wee bit dramatic, don't you think?" Alex asked as he grabbed Ridley's hand and entwined their fingers.

"Shooting water out your nose *is* a bit dramatic," Ridley grumbled and allowed Alex to lead him from the water. "Not to mention traumatic.

And you cheated, so you should have to do dishes." Ridley made sure to put a little whine in his tone and pushed out his bottom lip for good measure.

It didn't work. Alex rolled his eyes. "You look ridiculous." He leaned over and pecked Ridley on the cheek. "But I did cheat, so if you cook, I'll do dishes. Deal?"

"Deal," Ridley agreed. He didn't mind cooking, as long as he could do it in the microwave, but washing dishes? Not so much. There wasn't a lot he wouldn't do, even pout, to get out of the chore.

"DON'T EVEN think about it," Alex advised without looking up from rinsing the dishes.

"What?"

"If you snap me with that towel, I will beat your ass," Alex promised.

After a long pause, Ridley leaned his hip against the counter next to Alex, brows furrowed and towel in his hand. "What makes you think I was going to?"

"Oh I don't know, maybe the fact that you've tried nearly every day for the past two weeks," Alex surmised.

"Damn, I'm getting predictable."

"Getting?" Alex retorted, giving Ridley a disbelieving look.

"Okay, I am," Ridley chuckled. "But you do deserve it for making me cook covered in lake salt and gunk."

"I was hungry," Alex responded unapologetically.

"Yeah, yeah, yeah."

Alex set the last dish on the drying rack and turned off the tap. He grabbed the towel from Ridley, quickly dried his hands, and tossed the towel behind him. He slid his arms around Ridley's waist and pulled him close, burying his face in the side of Ridley's neck. "Forgive me?" he murmured against Ridley's shower-warmed skin before kissing his way up to Ridley's ear.

Ridley shuddered. "Mmmhmm," he moaned and tilted his head, giving Alex more room.

"Thought so," Alex chuckled and kissed Ridley on the nose before releasing him and heading to the fridge. "How about we spend the rest of the afternoon with a good movie and a couple of beers?"

"Okay, but I get to pick the movie," Ridley responded.

"Oh hell no you don't," Alex grunted and snatched a couple of beers before following Ridley, who had rushed out of the kitchen. Ridley had crappy taste in movies. The worst were the bad B zombie movies he insisted were cult classics and had to be watched several times to truly appreciate them. Having spent several agonizing hours watching them, Alex still didn't appreciate them nor see the appeal.

Ridley dove onto the couch and grabbed the remote. "Oh hell yes I do. I have the magic wand," he exclaimed happily as he held it up.

"You're such a child," Alex muttered as he sat next to the giggling man and handed him one of the beers. Alex twisted off the top on his bottle, slipped it between his thumb and index finger, and snapped, sending the cap flying across the room.

"And I'm the child?" Ridley asked with a snort.

"Yup," Alex said with a grin and tipped up his beer.

Thankfully there weren't any rotting walking corpse movies on. After running through every channel at least twice, Ridley finally gave up and turned it to the western channel. Once the program was settled on, it didn't take long for beer bottles to be set aside and bodies to move into what had become a familiar position—Alex stretched out on the couch, Ridley in Alex's arms with his head resting on Alex's chest.

Alex ran his hand over Ridley's head. He liked the way the short shaved sides tickled the tips of his fingers. In fact, there was a lot about Ridley he liked. He liked the way he and Ridley could laugh and tease each other, the easy companionship between them, and how well they worked together. Then there was the sex. Their physical relationship was over the fucking top. Alex had never felt so satisfied and content. He supposed his feeling could be attributed to the fact that for the first time in his life, he was making an effort to learn someone's body, their likes and dislikes, rather than a constant series of one-night stands. However, Alex knew it was more than that—it was Ridley.

The time he'd spent in Slater had sucked, but he hadn't ever really thought of himself as lonely. Now, Ridley could leave for an hour and Alex missed him. Alex kissed the top of Ridley's head. *What are you doing to me?* Ridley's response was to kiss Alex's tightening chest right over his heart.

Ah dammit. This couldn't end well. Eventually he would have to return to California, Ridley to Michigan, and they both would return to their previous lives. The idea made Alex's stomach sick and his heart hurt. He snuggled farther into the couch, wrapped his arms tighter around Ridley, and although he knew he shouldn't, he hoped their time here wouldn't end any time soon.

CHAPTER 22

ALEX BOLTED upright in bed, scanning the area as he strained to listen, but he neither heard nor saw anything that could explain what had pulled him from a sound sleep. Ridley made a snuffling noise next to him and then rolled and covered his head with the sheet. Alex's heart sped when he heard what must have disturbed his sleep—the sound of wood creaking, as if someone was walking on the front porch.

He retrieved his gun from beneath his pillow and silently left the bed, careful not to disturb Ridley. He crept down the hall, his senses hyperaware of any threats of danger. The sun was just beginning to rise, so he was able to take in his surroundings with ease. Unfortunately that meant whoever was out there would have a perfect sight line once he entered the living room.

Gun leading the way, Alex peeked around the corner and then let out a sigh of relief when he spotted Mick standing directly in front of the picture window, cell phone to his ear.

Alex flipped the safety on his gun to keep from shooting the bastard for scaring the shit out of him and set it on the coffee table as he stomped to the door. He threw it open. "Do you realize how close you came to getting a bullet in your ass?"

"Call you back," Mick said into his phone and ended the call. "There you go talking about my ass again." Mick tsked. "You really need to come to terms with the fact you can't have it."

Alex fought the urge to roll his eyes. "What the hell are you doing here?"

"You're going home," Mick said jubilantly and held out his fist.

"I'm what?" Alex asked in confusion.

"Dude, don't leave me hanging here," Mick complained, continuing to hold out his fist.

He didn't know what the hell Mick was talking about and slapped his hand away without bumping fists. "What the hell are you spouting off about?"

Mick looked down at his hand, frowning, and then shrugged. "Alvarez rolled."

"Gutierrez's lieutenant?" Alex asked dubiously.

"Yup. Apparently he got wind of a price on his head and turned over enough documentation to shut down the entire cartel just like that," Mick said with a snap of his fingers. "Your puny ass has lost its value."

Alex slumped back against the railing of the porch, grabbing it for support. "You've got to be shitting me?"

"Dead serious. Your ass ain't worth two cents." Mick smirked.

"I'm going home?" Alex muttered, overlooking the insult about his worth. *I'm going home?* He scrubbed a hand over his jaw and stared at his partner as if he'd grown two heads, the weirdness equivalent to the alien shit he was blathering on about. *Home? That's not possible.*

"Wow, that isn't quite the reaction I expected out of you," Mick sighed.

"Over? How in the hell can it be over?" Alex bristled.

"I thought you'd be happy."

"Over!" Alex pushed away from the railing. He narrowed his eyes and leaned closer to Mick. "How the fuck can it just be over?"

"What the hell, man?" Mick asked and took a step back.

Alex threw his hands up and stomped down the steps, anger bubbling up to the surface and skittering along his nerve endings like a flash fire. "That's it? All the buildup, the danger, the cloak-and-dagger bullshit." He spun around to face his partner—who was now looking at him as if he were the one who'd grown two heads—and pointed at his curls. "I had fucking wood shards in my goddamn hair, Mick!"

"You're losing it," Mick muttered with a shake of his head.

"I broke my mama's heart. My family and friends have thought I was dead for the last eighteen months and that's it?" Alex asked, not expecting an answer as he continued to stomp and fume and curse. "This is bullshit, Mick. Not to mention really fucking anticlimactic. What the hell kind of ending is that?"

"The kind of ending where you didn't get dead," Mick reminded him patiently.

"Alex! What's wrong?" Ridley called out as he came rushing out the front door. His gaze settled on Mick, and he slowly moved up close to Alex. "What's going on?" he asked cautiously.

"Alex is being a drama queen," Mick responded in exasperation. "How you doing, Ridley?"

Alex glared at his partner.

"I'm good." Ridley looked back and forth between Alex and Mick. "Someone want to tell me what's going on?"

"Be my guest," Mick said with flair, bowing to Alex.

Alex continued to glare at Mick as a rush of conflicting emotions went through him. Excitement, confusion, anger, relief all battled for the forefront, leaving him off balance and unsure of how he felt. Eighteen months of madness and it was over. Just like that? Over?

"Alex?" Ridley asked quietly as he laid a hand against the small of Alex's back.

Alex squeezed his eyes shut. "We're going home."

Alex felt Ridley stiffen next to him. "Excuse me?"

Alex blew out a breath and then another before turning to Ridley and meeting his confused gaze. "We're going home. Gutierrez's lieutenant turned state's evidence. The entire cartel is going down. Eddie Alvarez is taking our place in the witness protection program. We're going home."

Ridley's eyes went wide. "Seriously?"

"Think we can discuss this over coffee?" Mick chimed in. "I've been up for hours and haven't had a drop. I'm starting to get a little cranky."

Ridley continued to stare at Alex for a moment with a questioning expression on his face. Alex slid his arm around Ridley's waist. "I think coffee would be a good idea."

Ridley nodded and allowed Alex to lead him into the house. Ridley started the coffee, and Alex pulled three mugs from the cabinet. He set them on the island along with cream and sugar.

"All right, when did all this shit go down?" Alex asked Mick as he took a seat at the island.

"Three days ago Alvarez walked through the front door of the bureau carrying a big cardboard box and demanding protection."

"Just like that?" Alex muttered in disbelief. The reality of it was still hard to get his mind around.

"Yup, just like that. Alvarez was whisked away to an interrogation room, and once the bomb squad determined the box was safe, they discovered it was full of names, phone numbers, financial reports, and contracts, everything needed to completely crumble Gutierrez's empire."

"But why would he do that?" Ridley asked, bringing the pot of coffee to the island and pouring some in each mug.

"Gutierrez has always been quite a paranoid figure—"

"That's a nice way of saying the fucker is insane," Alex interrupted.

"Which is understandable," Mick agreed. "A man in his position constantly has to be looking over his shoulder for law enforcement as well as his criminal associates both within his cartel and out."

"I get that," Ridley acknowledged. "But Alvarez must have been trusted if he made it to such a high rank."

"Trust no one. Gutierrez has had eighteen months to ponder that," Mick said over the rim of his mug. He took a sip before continuing. "I'm guessing the longer Alvarez failed to eliminate their problem—Alex—the more Gutierrez began to suspect his lieutenant's capabilities as well as his loyalties.

"From what I've been told, after the unsuccessful attempt in Slater, Gutierrez put a price on Alvarez's head. Fearing for his life, Alvarez turned to us for protection."

"What does that mean for us?" Ridley asked, sounding wary.

"It means you get to go home," Mick replied with a broad smile. "It's over."

The disbelief and unease once again skittered along Alex's nerve endings. It shouldn't bother him how Gutierrez went down. It was, after all, the reason he'd been in hiding, the takedown of the cartel his only goal. Still, he couldn't help but feel as if he'd been cheated out of the privilege of being the one to do it. A slap to his ego? Perhaps, or maybe he simply felt as if he'd spent the last eighteen months hiding for nothing.

Alex glanced sidelong at Ridley, who was staring silently at Mick with a shocked expression as he drank his coffee.

"Jesus Christ," Mick grumbled after the silence had gone on for long moments. "I thought I'd get a little more reaction than this out of you two. What the hell, man?"

Ridley met Alex's gaze, and in that moment Alex realized what was bothering him so much. Yes, it was in large part due to being denied the chance to take Gutierrez down, but another part, a personal portion, said he wasn't ready to leave Hackberry or Ridley. Alex was pretty sure Ridley was thinking the same thing by the look of sadness he caught in his man's eyes. However, with Mick looking back and forth between Alex and Ridley expectantly, it wasn't the time or the place to discuss it.

Alex turned away from Ridley and met his partner's gaze. "Okay, so where do we go from here?"

"You and I leave for home in about—" Mick checked his watch. "—an hour."

Alex's gut roiled. "That soon? What about Ridley? I don't want to leave him here alone."

"That's up to Ridley," Mick responded with a shrug and looked to Ridley. "You can fly out the same time as us or extend your vacation. The house is yours to use for however long you'd like and we'll provide you with protection until we are one hundred percent certain there is no longer any threat to you."

"What about me?" Alex demanded. "Why the hell can't I extend my vacation and be his protection?"

Mick gave him an exasperated look. "Because the higher-ups, you know, the ones who sign your paycheck, want your cranky little ass back home for debriefing."

"I...." Ridley cleared his throat, his voice low when he said, "I think I'd prefer to go home now. Can I call my family?"

"Sure," Mick said with a gentle smile. "Use the secure cell I left for you. I'm sure they will be relieved to hear from you."

"Thanks," Ridley muttered and, without looking at Alex, left the room.

Alex watched him go, a heaviness settling in his chest causing it to ache. He wasn't ready to say good-bye, wasn't ready to leave their little hideaway. For the first time in his adult life, Alex was truly happy, content, and felt complete. He didn't want it to end, not yet. Maybe never.

"Dude, what the hell is wrong with you?" Mick asked, concern evident in his tone.

Alex couldn't respond with the lump that had formed in his throat, and he didn't dare meet his partner's gaze, at least not until his eyes stopped burning from unshed tears.

RIDLEY BLEW out the breath he was holding as he entered the bedroom. He slumped down on the edge of the mattress when his shaking legs began to go weak. He'd known this moment would come, but had done his best to block it from his thoughts. Now his happy bubble had popped and he felt numb.

He rested his forearms on his knees and hung his head. He knew he should be rushing to the phone and calling his parents, but he simply couldn't bring himself to do it yet. He needed a moment, as selfish as it was, to sort through his feelings. From the moment he'd witnessed Alex rush out the door under a hail of gunfire, it had been like one big surreal adventure, a fantasy. He'd been able to lock away the guilt he felt for his parents' plight along with the fear of danger, and he'd had the best time of his life with Alex.

What would happen next? Would he ever see Alex again once he returned to California and Ridley went home to Michigan? How the hell was he supposed to go back to being the typical college kid with homework, exams, tiny little apartment with no room, no excitement—and no Alex?

One hour was all he had left.

Ridley scrubbed both hands over his face and gave himself a little internal shake. If he had so little time left, he'd be damned if he was going to spend it hiding in his room moping and whining. Time to man up.

Ridley pushed up from the bed and went to the nightstand where he'd stored his cell phone and pulled it out. Returning to the bed, he sat back down on the edge of the mattress and dialed the familiar number.

"Hello," his mom's voice came through the phone line.

"Mom, it's Ridley."

"Oh dear sweet Jesus, Ridley." His mom sobbed. "Where have you been? We've been so worried. We thought—" She choked on a sob and could only cry into the phone.

Ridley's chest tightened. "Shh, Mom, it's okay. I'm okay. I'm coming home and I'll explain everything."

"When?" she squeaked out between sobs.

"I'll be home later today. I'll call when I get to the airport. Mom... shh...," he murmured soothingly as she continued to weep. "Is Dad there?"

"No, he's at work."

"Listen to me. I'm going to hang up so I can pack. You call Dad and give him the good news, okay? Can you do that?"

"Yes. Oh, Ridley. I've been so scared. So worried." She began crying harder, great sobs, but was finally able to say, "I thought you were dead."

"I know, and I'm sorry. But I'll explain everything when I get there."

Ridley rubbed at the ache in his chest as his mom continued to cry and waited patiently until she was able to speak again. "Okay. I love you," she sniffled.

"I love you too. I'll see you soon."

Ridley disconnected the call and wiped the tears from his eyes. Hearing the pain in his mom's voice, knowing it was his fault, shredded his heart. Somehow he'd have to make it up to her and his dad.

Ridley tossed the phone aside and headed for the shower. He washed and dressed as quickly as he could. He then packed up his meager belongings in a duffel bag and went to find Alex.

Ridley found him and Mick sitting on the front porch. They both looked up as he stepped out the door. "I'll give you two a minute alone," Mick offered, getting to his feet.

Ridley sat on the step next to Alex, watching Mick walk to his car. "It's been a hell of an adventure," Ridley said somberly, still watching Mick.

"That it has," Alex responded and wrapped an arm around Ridley's waist, resting his hand on Ridley's hip. The familiar gesture caused the vise around Ridley's heart to tighten further.

Ridley struggled to find something to say, but words eluded him. It hadn't been that long ago that he'd told Alex he wasn't looking for commitment. He'd believed it at the time. Before coming to Hackberry, he'd been happy in his carefree life as an unattached college student with the added bonus of a fuck buddy. Now it didn't matter what he wanted. Alex would be returning to his old life and Ridley back to his.

"Did you get hold of your mom?" Alex asked, his thumb caressing Ridley's hip.

"Yeah. It sucked hearing her cry, ya know, but...." Ridley shrugged. "She'll be okay now. Did you call yours?"

"Nah, I figured after all this time, they wouldn't believe it until they actually saw me. I'm going to walk through the door, bend over, and take the ass whipping like a man," Alex chuckled.

A heavy silence fell over them. It was thick and suffocating and nothing like the silence when they were stretched out on the lounge chair watching the sun set. This was different, full of sadness and uncertainty.

Alex must have felt it too because after about ten minutes, he patted Ridley's hip. "I won't ever regret bringing you into this," he whispered. Alex pressed a soft kiss to Ridley's temple. "I'm going to miss you."

Ridley couldn't respond nor could he find the strength to stop Alex as he stood and headed up the steps. Ridley sat there long after Alex had entered the house, the numbness that had seeped into him when he first found out he was going home keeping his emotions from spilling out his eyes.

He was still silently numb when they went their separate ways at the airport.

WEEK 1

DID YOU make it home?
    The text went unanswered.

WEEK 2

"HI ALEX, it's Ridley. I'm getting worried. You haven't been replying to my text messages. Things are going pretty good here. Mom and Dad are glad to have me back, but.... Well.... I can't stop thinking about you. I really miss—"

Beep

Alex didn't respond to the message.

WEEK 3

AFTER LEAVING yet another message, Ridley lay on his bed staring at the ceiling, cell phone resting on his chest.

Alex didn't call.

EPILOGUE

A SOFT rap on his bedroom door was followed by his mom's quiet voice. "Ridley?"

In the month since he'd been back home, his mom had treated him much as she had when he was a small child, constantly checking on him, cooking his favorite meals, and each night she'd come in to his room to give him a hug, kiss his head, and whisper *I love you* before she headed to bed.

He wasn't used to being smothered, but he wasn't complaining either. She'd been devastated when she'd learned he was missing. The not knowing whether he was alive or dead for nearly three months had aged her ten years, as it had his dad. She deserved the chance to coddle her only child for a while.

"The door's open," he called out and grinned when she opened the door a crack and peeked in before pushing it open and entering. He wasn't sure what she thought he'd be doing since he'd told her to come in, but he found it endearing.

His mom looked a bit pale and she was wringing her hands nervously. His mom, once a bubbly, happy-go-lucky soul, was now a shell of what she used to be. Ridley would forever regret causing the damage he'd done to his parents' psyche, and he could only pray that once they dealt with the pain their previous personalities would once again shine brighter than their anguish.

Ridley jumped to his feet, instantly worried. "What's the matter?"

"There's someone at the door asking for you."

"It's okay, Mom," he said soothingly as he wrapped an arm around her and hugged her. "If they were here to do me harm, do you really think they would knock on the door first?"

He felt his mom began to shake, and when he looked down at her, he realized she was laughing silently. "I'm such a dork."

Ridley kissed her forehead. "Nah, it's called being a mom and I love you for it. So let's go see who's at the door, shall we?"

"He's a very nice-looking young man, with the cutest blond curls," his mom commented with a slight grin. "Maybe he's one of your admirers."

"I don't have admirers," Ridley snorted. "Ah," he hushed her when she opened her mouth to speak. "And no, I don't want one, so stop trying to play matchmaker."

One of the new aspects to his mom's personality was nagging him about finding a nice guy to settle down with, get married, kids, white picket fence, dog tied in the backyard. It was the same thing most parents wanted for their kids, and the fact that he was gay didn't change her all-American dream for him. Sure, he could have all those things one day if he was so inclined, but at this point in his life, none of it was all that appealing to him. He'd much rather have crazy adventures with.... *Wait a minute.* Ridley's heart sped.

"Did you say blond curls?"

"Yes. It's—"

Ridley didn't wait to hear what else she was about to say. He tore out of his room, heart hammering. It couldn't be him. He hadn't received so much as a text from Alex since they'd said their quick, awkward good-bye, but the slight chance, as improbable as it was, had him taking the stairs two at a time. In his haste he missed the last step and went crashing into the front door with a painful crack as his shoulder hit wood.

"Ow! Son of a hitchhiker. Ow!" He grabbed his shoulder, wincing in pain.

"Better watch that last step, it's a doozy."

Ridley spun around. Leaning against the entry into the study was the most amazingly beautiful head of blond curls he'd ever seen.

He didn't even give it a second thought. Ridley took the two long strides that separated them and, ignoring the pain in his shoulder, pulled back his arm and let it fly, landing a punch to Alex's right shoulder.

"Jesus Christ, Ridley. What the hell was that for?" Alex grumbled as he rubbed the spot.

The punch hadn't been hard enough to send the man backward, but he damn sure got the message across. "An entire month, Alex. No call, no e-mail, not even a goddamn text to let me know you were okay. Do you have any idea how worried I've been?"

"I think someone missed me," Alex responded smugly with a teasing grin curling his lip.

"Ridley? Is everything okay?" his mom called out as she came rushing down the stairs.

"I'm fine, Mom," he assured her without looking away from Alex's laughing gaze.

"Sarah Corbin, Alex Castren. He's the guy—"

"I know who Alex Castren is," his mom squealed and rushed to hug Alex. "Thank you for keeping my son safe."

Alex's expression changed from smug to uncomfortable, and he awkwardly patted her back. "Umm. You're welcome?"

"You'll stay for dinner, won't you? Richie would be heartbroken if he didn't get a chance to meet you and thank you himself."

"Of course he'll stay," Ridley answered for him, shooting Alex a challenging look.

"Wonderful," his mom exclaimed excitedly and clapped her hands together as she took a step back. "Any preferences? I've got a roast in the oven but if you'd prefer something else…."

"Roast sounds absolutely perfect," Alex said with a gentle smile. "Thank you for the offer."

"Ridley, don't be rude. Take our guest's coat and offer him something to drink." She swatted Ridley on the butt as she headed out of the room, undoubtedly to the kitchen. "I raised him better than that," she tossed over her shoulder, winking at Alex.

"She's cute," Alex chuckled.

"Yeah, just don't piss her off. So what the hell, man? You couldn't take a few seconds to contact me in the last month?" Ridley grumbled, steering them back to the conversation he'd started.

Alex rubbed his arm again, the smug grin once again showing itself. "So, are you going to admit you missed me?"

"Of course I missed you, you shithead. I love you." Ridley's eyes went wide and his heart stopped dead in his chest. He'd known since they'd been in Hackberry that he was in love with Alex. Hell, probably even before then, but he hadn't said it out loud. He damn sure hadn't meant to blurt it out now.

"Really?" Alex asked without a shred of shock in his tone. "You love me?"

"I, um…. Stop trying to change the subject," he muttered in a feeble attempt to avoid the question.

Alex stepped up close and grabbed Ridley's hip, curling his fingers in the cotton material of Ridley's sweat pants. Alex held Ridley's gaze, an intense shine in his gunmetal-blue eyes. Damn, how he'd missed looking into those amazing eyes. He'd missed Alex's intense gaze, that smug smile, his touch, his voice, his heat.

Alex ran his other hand along Ridley's cheek, and he pushed into the touch, eyes threatening to flutter closed. "I'm sorry," Alex said regretfully. "They've kept me locked down in debriefing. I wasn't able to contact anyone until they were one hundred percent sure there was no further threat. The second I was released, I headed to the airport and came here." Alex pressed his mouth against Ridley's, speaking against his lips. "Forgive me?"

"A whole month," Ridley moaned and kissed him back, wrapping an arm around Alex's waist and pulling him closer.

"What if I told you I loved you too?" he asked in between kisses. "Would you forgive me then?"

Hearing Alex say he loved him caused Ridley's belly to flip-flop and his body to thrum. A lump formed in this throat with the well of emotions, stealing his ability to speak. He chased Alex's lips, licking and tasting the flavor he'd missed so much and steered them back until he could catch the door to the study with his foot. The second it clicked shut, he spun Alex and pinned him against the wall.

"Maybe," he moaned and deepened the kiss.

Ridley explored every inch of Alex's mouth while he stroked, touched, and kneaded every inch of Alex's body he could reach. The taut muscles of his back and ass, lean hips, flat belly, firm chest, all got attention while he feasted upon Alex's mouth. Warmth rushed through him, his cock beginning to swell, but this wasn't about sex, although the idea was more than a little appealing. This was about something more than physical. The kiss and touch was all about welcoming Alex back, saying *I've missed you* and *don't ever fucking leave me again.*

He had memorized this body. Calling up the vivid images of Alex, the dreams of him here with Ridley, were what had gotten him through the last month of being without Alex. He knew every bump and ridge and scar, but he needed to reacquaint himself with this cocky, smug, crude-mouthed, stubborn bastard he'd fallen utterly and irrevocably in love with.

Ridley was breathless when he ended the kiss, and he buried his face in the warm flesh of Alex's neck, inhaling deeply, taking in Alex's intoxicating scent.

Alex slid his hand through Ridley's hair and held him close. "I really am sorry I couldn't call. I've been going nuts without you. I've missed you so fucking much."

"I've missed you too."

They both seemed content to hold each other, touching and breathing each other in. No words were needed at the moment. A loud bang from the area of the kitchen brought them back from where they were and they both jumped.

"C'mon, we better get in there and see if we can help before she comes looking for us. We can talk later, yeah?" Ridley asked.

"I'm not going anywhere. Especially with pot roast in the oven."

Ridley leaned in and gave Alex one last quick kiss and then started to open the door. Alex stopped him by taking his hand. "How much do they know about us? I don't want to do anything that makes your mom uncomfortable."

"I haven't told her everything, but she knows we had a relationship while on the run. She's cool with it."

"And your dad?"

"Just be yourself and he'll either love you or want to slap you upside the head. Like father, like son," he said wryly.

"I'll be on my best behavior."

Ridley led Alex to the kitchen without releasing his hand. Just before they entered, Alex leaned in and whispered, "At least until we're alone."

Ridley shivered.

"Hey, Mom, anything we can do to help?"

His mom glanced down at their entwined hands and smiled broadly. "You can set the table. Alex, you're our guest, have a seat," she ordered and pulled out a chair. "Can I get you something to drink?"

"No thank you, ma'am, and I don't mind helping out."

"Please call me Sarah and I insist," she said, holding the back of the chair.

"I wouldn't argue with her," Ridley advised as he pulled a stack of plates from the cupboard. "Remember what I said about pissing her off."

"Don't listen to a word he says. Now sit," she told him in that mom tone that could still instill fear in Ridley's inner child.

Alex, being the smart man he was, sat.

As Ridley set the table, he took every opportunity to brush up against Alex. They were both smiling like fools as Ridley's mom went on and on about whatever it was she was talking about. Ridley tried to pay attention as she gave Alex the third degree, asking him about his parents, job, what it was like growing up in California, blah, blah blah. Ridley was too busy struggling to keep from grabbing the sexy man and rushing him off to his room and locking the door, or better yet, out the door and to a hotel room where they wouldn't have to be quiet.

No, no, no, he silently chastised himself. Unless he wanted to totally embarrass himself in front of his parents, no naughty thoughts.

"Sarah, I'm home," Ridley's dad called out from the foyer.

"Perfect timing," Mom murmured as she pulled the roast from the oven. "You boys wash your hands."

"Yes, ma'am," they said in unison and bumped shoulders as they fought to wash their hands at the same time.

"Whose black car is in the drive?" his dad asked as he entered the kitchen. Then he spotted Alex. "Oh, hi."

"This is Alex," his mom said, rushing to her husband and giving him a peck on the cheek. "He's the boy who kept our Ridley safe."

Alex stepped forward, hand extended. "Alex Castren. Nice to meet you, sir."

"Rich Corbin," his dad replied huskily, the well of emotion evident in the expression on his face.

Ridley wished he could have seen the look on Alex's face— undoubtedly it was priceless—when instead of shaking the offered hand, his dad grabbed it and pulled Alex to him and gave him a hug.

"Dad, let the poor man breathe," Ridley laughed.

"Sorry," his dad said and patted Alex on the back a couple of times before releasing him. "It's damn good to finally meet you, son. It means a lot to us what you did for our boy."

"Nice to meet you too, sir," Alex said, looking a little uneasy as he glanced at Ridley.

"Please, call me Rich."

Alex looked relieved when he once again took a seat. Ridley sat next to him and laid his hand on Alex's thigh, giving it a little squeeze. His parents had always been huggers. They could be a little overwhelming at first, but they were good people and would have Alex totally comfortable around them in no time.

And he was. Alex was patient, answering all the same questions Mom had asked him and smiling at Dad the entire time. It was Ridley who couldn't get comfortable. It was seriously the most painful dinner he'd endured. The food was wonderful, his mom was a great cook and normally pot roast was his favorite, but he was going mad. Alex's leg was pressed against his, he kept getting whiffs of Alex's scent, and no matter how hard he tried, he couldn't stop looking at Alex and wishing they were somewhere else.

Ridley sighed internally when his mom finally stood and picked up her plate. "Can I get anyone coffee with their dessert?" she offered.

Ugh, not dessert. Ridley shot a pleading look at Alex, willing the man to decline dessert.

"Actually, would you mind if we waited a bit on dessert?" Alex asked as he wiped his mouth and set his napkin on his empty plate. "I have something I'd like to show Ridley. It will only take an hour, tops."

He was so going to kiss Alex for that.

"Oh, no. No problem at all," his mom replied as she picked up the dishes. "I'm sure you and Ridley have plenty to catch up on. We can have dessert another time. You will come back again, won't you?"

"Yes, ma'am." Alex smiled.

Ridley took a stack of dishes to the sink.

"Just leave them on the counter," Mom said. "I'll get your father to help with the dishes. You two run along."

"You sure? I don't mind helping."

"Go," Mom ordered and pecked Ridley on the cheek. "Go have fun."

"Thanks." Ridley kissed her back and whispered, "Love ya."

"Love ya too," she responded and patted his cheek.

"It was great to finally meet you, Alex. Come back anytime," Dad said and hugged Alex again.

Numerous hugs and promises to come again later, Ridley finally pried Alex from his parents' grip and rushed him out the door.

"Your parents are great."

"Uh-huh" was Ridley's only response until he was sitting in the passenger seat of Alex's rental car. "I'm warning you right now, whatever you plan on showing me better be a bed," Ridley growled.

Alex didn't answer, simply put the car in gear, but the smirk on his face was telling. Alex was as insatiable as Ridley, and after a month apart, Ridley was confident they were heading to a hotel. He only hoped Alex had picked one that was close by.

Alex obviously had the same thought or could read Ridley's mind, but still, Ridley was thrumming, his heart slamming in his chest, and his cock rock hard when they pulled into the Holiday Inn five minutes later.

They were barely through the door before Alex was on him, but that was okay because Ridley was doing his best to move into Alex's arms, needing the contact. The back of Ridley's legs hit the mattress, and he pulled Alex down with him onto the bed with one hand tangled in Alex's curls and the other on his hip.

The weight on top of Ridley was familiar and welcomed. The slide of lips became a fierce, possessive kiss, a clash of lips and tongues and teeth. Hands frantically pulled at shirts and pants, each pawing the other as well as trying to shimmy and shift to help facilitate the removal and trying to kick off shoes.

Alex pulled back from the kiss long enough to pull his T-shirt over his head. "Damn, I missed you," he said as he tossed his shirt aside and dove back in.

"Missed you too," Ridley moaned into Alex's mouth. God, how he had missed him. The worry and sadness and doubt drained from Ridley's heart as it swelled with so much love and happiness he felt as if it would burst right out of his chest.

He wasn't sure how they were able to do it with fumbling and frantic hands, but they ended up naked in the center of the bed, Alex straddling Ridley's hips. They moved together, breathing each other in as hands continued to explore and touch. Ridley soaked in the heat of Alex's body, the need and want rising as quickly as the fire blazing between them.

Ridley put his hands on Alex's hips, fingers curling as he encouraged Alex to move. Low moans came from both of them as they began to rock.

Ridley slid his mouth along Alex's jaw, breathing harshly. He licked at the soft spot below Alex's ear. "Need you so much," he whispered.

Alex shuddered above him and slid his hands under Ridley's arms to grip his shoulders. Alex groaned, nuzzling the side of Ridley's neck as they continued to move against each other.

Their movements became more frantic, rocking and thrusting. Hands clutched so hard they bruised flesh, and cocks slid, painting long-denied need and passion along the other. Ridley wanted to crawl inside Alex, never let him go.

Alex cried out Ridley's name as his body tensed and jerked. When he bit down on Ridley's shoulder and muttered "love you," Ridley's control was shredded. One last shuddering breath and Ridley came, shouting out Alex's name, "love you," "missed you," and words of nonsense. He held Alex until the tension released its grip and he melted into the mattress, spent.

They lay there wrapped in each other's arms as they came down from their high. For the first time in a month, Ridley felt complete.

Alex rolled them until they were lying on their sides facing each other.

"I was beginning to think I'd never see you again," Ridley admitted quietly. He reached up and brushed a wayward curl from Alex's cheek. "So glad you came."

"I'm sorry. I wanted to, honest. It was the longest month of my life. You have to know you were never far from my thoughts. Jesus, Ridley. I couldn't eat or sleep or fucking breathe without thinking about you. Wanted nothing more than to get back to you."

"You don't know how ridiculously happy that makes me." Ridley pressed a soft kiss to Alex's lips, smiling against his mouth.

Alex pushed up and leaned on his elbow. "I don't want to be without you again. Ever. I've asked for a transfer. I put in for two different locations and all I need is for you to tell me which one to take."

Ridley stared at him in disbelief. "Really?" he asked past the lump in his throat.

Alex nodded. "Yeah, really. One is close to Slater, about an hour away, but I could commute while you finished your degree."

"You'd hate being a Yooper," Ridley chuckled.

"I'd do it for you. I know I didn't say it—didn't even realize it until we were apart—but I want to start and end every day with you in my arms."

"I feel the same way," Ridley murmured huskily as he blinked back tears of relief and joy. "Where's the other job?"

"Well, it would require me to travel for assignments from time to time, but when I was home we could even work together. And the weather is a whole lot better than in Slater," Alex said vaguely.

"And?"

"And I have a house all picked out. I talked to the owner and he's more than happy to sell it to us at a really reasonable rate."

"Dammit, Alex, would you just tell me?" Ridley huffed.

"It's got this most amazing deck with these really wide loungers where we could watch the sun set every night."

Ridley's breath caught. "You...." He cleared his throat, the excitement bubbling up causing his voice to crack. "You want to move to Hackberry?"

Alex nodded and Ridley shoved him onto his back, crawling on top of him and peppering his face with kisses. "Oh my fucking God!"

"I take it you like option two," Alex chuckled.

"Yes! Yes! Yes! I can transfer universities, adjust my schedule to work around fishing." His heart was hammering. Jesus he'd missed their time together in Hackberry. He'd spent hours dreaming of being back there, spending his life there living, loving, and working alongside Alex. "When do we leave?"

"As soon as you're ready," Alex got out between snorts of laughter as Ridley continued to cover his face with kisses.

"Just give me enough time to tell Mom and Dad and pack a bag."

Alex rolled them again, landing on top and looked down at Ridley, his smile fading. "Okay, but one more thing."

"What is it?" Ridley asked uneasily at the seriousness in Alex's tone.

"I'm the captain. Got it, matey?"

Ridley grabbed a handful of curls and smashed their mouths together in a bruising kiss without answering. He had no issues with letting Alex be the captain. Alex may be a badass motherfucker, but Ridley was a badass first mate, and he knew exactly how to commandeer the captain's vessel.

SJD PETERSON, better known as Jo, hails from Michigan. Not the best place to live for someone who hates the cold and snow. When not reading or writing, Jo can be found close to the heater checking out NHL stats and watching the Red Wings kick a little butt. Can't cook, misses the clothes hamper nine out of ten tries, but is handy with power tools.

Visit Jo at:

http://www.facebook.com/SJD.Peterson;
http://sjdpeterson.blogspot.com/;https://twitter.com/SJDPeterson;

and http://www.goodreads.com/author/show/4563849.S_J_D_Peterson.

Contact Jo at sjdpeterson@gmail.com.

Guards of Folsom Series from SJD PETERSON

http://www.dreamspinnerpress.com

Whispering Pines Ranch from SJD PETERSON

http://www.dreamspinnerpress.com

Whispering Pines Ranch from SJD PETERSON

http://www.dreamspinnerpress.com

Also from SJD PETERSON

BEYOND
DUTY
SJD Peterson

http://www.dreamspinnerpress.com

Also from SJD PETERSON

Also from SJD PETERSON

SJD PETERSON

MASTERS & BOYD

Also from SJD PETERSON

http://www.dreamspinnerpress.com

Also from SJD PETERSON

A WHISPERING PINES RANCH SHORT

SJD PETERSON

http://www.dreamspinnerpress.com